SILLY

SILLY MOTHERS

Short stories by

Catherine Merriman

H O N N O *M O D E R N   F I C T I O N*

Published by Honno
'Ailsa Craig' Heol y Cawl Dinas Powys
South Glamorgan CF6 4AH
First Impression 1991
© *Catherine Merriman 1991*

British Library Cataloguing in Publication Data

Merriman, Catherine 1949 –
Silly mothers
I. Title
823 . 914 [F]

ISBN 1-870206-10-X

Published with the financial support of the Welsh Arts Council

Acknowledgements

The following stories from this collection have already appeared in print:
'Silly Mothers' in *New England Review*, 1988; 'The Secret' in *Iron Women* (Iron Press), 1990;
'Painting Pylons' in *New Welsh Review*, 1988; 'The Husbag' in *Writing Women*, 1989
and *Everywoman*, 1991; 'Ballad of a Desperate Man' in *Argo*, 1991.

Cover illustration by Wendy Sinclair
Designed by Ruth Dineen

Typeset in Palatino by Megaron, Cardiff
Printed by Gwasg John Penry, Swansea

CONTENTS

SILLY MOTHERS

Sarah was a dreamer. When she was a little girl, and even not so little, her school reports had remarked on it. They had said, at first indulgently: Sarah has a short attention span; and later, less indulgently: Sarah will get better results when she learns to concentrate; which Sarah used to think unfair, because she did concentrate, she concentrated extremely well, only on the wrong things. Words bounced off her easily; but pictures, images, the desperate messages etched in the surface of her desk, the heroes in her head – they held her full attention. Now, a generation on, she was just as good at it. She dreamed as she ironed her husband's shirts, hoovered the carpets; dreamed as she changed the baby's nappy, rinsed his plastic pants; even dreamed as she waited outside the school for Thomas, if she were allowed to, the baby in the pushchair and Louise exploring the grounds, if Louise didn't suddenly announce she had to go to the toilet, eager to go where the big girls went, knowing she would get her way. When Louise had to go, she had to go.

Sometimes Sarah thought she dreamed too much. Sometimes she turned the radio on as she ironed, or washed up, and was relieved if it caught her, made her listen. Sometimes she talked to the baby, instead of simply hugging him, or smiling at him, but not for long. She found the effort of forming the words a strain, difficult to sustain for more than a minute or two when she could expect no reply. She talked to Louise, or rather Louise talked to her, incessantly, but Louise went to playschool, she still slept in the afternoons; there were hours when there was no one. And there was really nothing wrong with dreaming. She still heard the phone, or the baby cry, she didn't get lost in it. What harm could it do?

But she tried not to dream when her husband was around; he found it irritating. He would say to Thomas, 'Make sure Mummy's got her hearing aid in,' and Thomas would laugh, and so would she, and then say, 'What? Sorry, I was miles away,' and her husband would roll his eyes and repeat whatever it was so slowly and patiently she would start to worry she might slip off again before he reached the point. She could feel herself urging him on, willing him to catch her interest quickly, so she would be securely, undividedly back.

Occasionally he asked what she was thinking about, and if she couldn't invent anything practical fast enough she said, 'Oh nothing,' and it would almost be true, because being asked often made her forget. She didn't want to share her thoughts. A long time ago she had innocently told him a dream, in some detail. It was only a small dream, nothing too exciting, but it became even less exciting put into words. They were the wrong medium, they didn't capture the essence. Her husband had appeared baffled, he seemed to expect better of her, and she had never been able to use that dream again, its cover had been blown. So now she would only tell him what she didn't dream about. He had once asked her if she dreamed about him – almost coyly, as if he assumed her dreams were much more daring than in fact they were – and she had replied, 'No, of course not,' and been surprised to see he was a little hurt. She had said, 'But I never dream about what I've already got,' because it seemed obvious to her. Whoever heard of millionaires dreaming of riches, or married women of weddings? Or if they did, they were thinking, or remembering, or planning; not dreaming.

She had to find faces for her dreams. Not all her characters needed them, some could be faceless, if they had only minor parts to play, but heroes needed faces, specific faces, and she couldn't invent them. Few men in real life were suitable. Either she knew them too well, which exempted them – they had their own lives, it made her feel guilty to exploit them – or she only saw them once, which wasn't enough. Anyway, dream men had to be very special, and few men in real life deserved a place in her dreams. So mostly she used faces from the television; they were ideal – faces, nothing more, and would do anything she devised for them. But she was always looking, because nobody lasted forever. Her story lines changed, and they often didn't carry over well. They seemed to have been spoilt by their previous history; or sometimes she went off them, or forgot exactly what they looked like; faces are difficult to hold for long, even in constant use.

Her dreams, she knew now, were very tame. She had read a book about womens' fantasies once; right up her street, her husband observed drily, seeing her deep in it. She read the book with incredulity. I never dream anything like this, she thought, they're joking, someone's having someone else on. How could anyone think such thoughts and not die with shame? It disturbed her, made her feel immature and unadventurous. If other women allowed themselves thoughts like this . . . well! She cautiously pushed her own dreams a little further, but panicked immediately. She couldn't make her heroes do that! And especially not if they had real faces. She would use them, but responsibly, she didn't want anyone hurt. And then she had giggled to herself, thinking how free the space in her head was, but still she couldn't do it. I'm satisfied with very little, she told herself. That's a sign of sanity – she had read it somewhere – I don't have to feel inadequate because outrageous things don't happen in my fantasies. It's depth and quality I'm after, not lurid sensationalism and wild excitement. Well, there was excitement of course, but a subtle excitement, an excitement of nuance: in the turn of a head, an angle of view; not in anything as crude as mere activity. She could dwell on one unmoving scene for hours, filling it out until she had got it exactly, perfectly, right. She should have been a photographer, she decided, images were what she was good at. A story was necessary, to give the whole thing purpose, but it was the images that mattered. Indeed quite often she never saw the end of the stories at all, they remained vague and unrealized. She had spent too much time on the images as she travelled; she was interrupted long before the conclusion was in sight.

When Thomas started his Thursday piano lessons, straight after school, she found a real face. He worked in the ironmongers. She spent the half hour·of the lesson there; it was a great barn of a place, easy to browse in, its shelves packed with everything from china to grass seed, power drills to dog baskets. While she dawdled she bought the dried dog food, which she could have bought in bulk, but which would have then given her nothing to do at all, because half an hour wasn't long enough to make it round the supermarket next door; she did that afterwards, with the other late-afternoon shoppers.

He ran the Do-It-Yourself section, really, but often helped out elsewhere. One of the other assistants would call, 'Hey, over here, William, just serve this lady while I'm busy,' and he would come smiling over and lean across the counter, attentive, as if what you were going to say was something delightful, something he couldn't wait to hear. And then he would say, 'Right, coming up,' and hand over whatever it was, triumphantly, like a present, a treat he had specially organized, just for you. He was extraordinarily beautiful; effortlessly, negligently beautiful, you knew he had never had to try. He wore tee-shirts or shirts open at the throat and rolled to the elbow; he had strong bare arms, no jewellery, nothing to show he cared. His hair was dark and wavy and as confident as he was, he tossed it around and ran his hand through it as if it didn't matter a jot, it had always behaved itself, always fell exactly where it looked best. And although he was young, he didn't look boyish. She didn't like boyish men, or rather, couldn't use them. Hers had to be grown-up men, capable of looking after themselves. William could look after anything. He was the son of the owner of the shop — she had heard him call Mr Jennings 'Dad'. One day it might all be his; perhaps that was why he was so interested, and enjoyed himself so much. She had never seen anyone so perfect in real life; he enthralled her. Before the glass door had swung to behind her she knew exactly where he was. At any moment, with her back to him, she could have turned and pointed straight at him. Even when she was talking to another assistant she could picture him, bending, stretching, propping himself carelessly against the counter, a thumb stuck into the front pocket of his jeans as he chatted, smiling confidentially at his customers; when she turned to see him, there he was, doing just as she imagined.

She began to toy with the idea that he noticed her. She rarely spoke to him, because it flustered her. She would hang back from the pet-food counter if it were busy, in case he was called over to serve her. But she could hardly believe her thoughts were undetectable, that they didn't radiate from her, and couldn't touch him. The notion excited her and she pursued it, when she could; it was annoying how often other women customers seemed to be with him, getting in the way. She hadn't noticed them before; now they started to irritate her. She began to despise how they smiled and laughed and monopolized his attention. Some of them even called him William, flaunting their familiarity; it seemed an embarrassing liberty, a crass announcement to the world of their claim to a stake in him. She could never have done such a thing, demeaned herself so. She felt herself superior, imagined her aloofness was her trump card, that he noticed her because she kept her messages private, between the two of them. But she had to be on her own, make space between herself and the children. It didn't work with them; they somehow unsexed her, stood between herself and her femininity, blocking the messages. She didn't understand why this should be, when sex led to children, but accepted it as fact. Children and messages didn't mix.

So when she went to the ironmongers she started to park the pushchair in a corner – somewhere interesting, somewhere the baby would like – and then wander round with just Louise, whom she didn't have to hold, and who sometimes could even be persuaded to stay and entertain the baby. When that happened she was delighted; she had her chance to feel truly free, and light, and female. She could imagine signals flashing both ways then. She knew they weren't, knew it rationally, but she could imagine them, they had credibility. She felt natural, womanly, receptive, independent; for a few minutes she could forget she was really a mother. Women on their own were allowed to be aware of men, to think of them, to send and receive messages: she remembered it, and what fun it was. Of course it was all a game, she knew that, but it was an important game; a game she needed.

And when it was over and she left the shop, still supersensitive and image-laden, she would collect Thomas and talk to the children as she strode towards the weekly shopping, making up for her moments of disloyalty, invigorated, almost ingratiating. It became a treat for them, she bought them off, literally, with the only sweets of the week, and figuratively, with her extra attention and patience. She was nicer to her husband when she got home, despite the rush to get everything unpacked and a meal prepared all in the brief hour before he returned. She would touch him and kiss him and say, 'Oh, what a day, the supermarket was heaving,' looking bright and exhilarated and as if breathlessness agreed with her. She gave up trying to persuade him to take her shopping in the car on Saturdays instead, as if by taking away this little atonement, the long haul home, pushchair creaking with bags, she might risk losing her earlier pleasures. And then she was restocked with William, as well as with food. She liked this notion, it made her laugh. And because she loved her husband, whom she had in real life and therefore didn't need to dream about, it was quite all right. There was nothing to feel guilty about. She even wondered whom her husband used in his thoughts: she liked to think everybody used someone. She knew her husband loved her, so that was all right as well. It was only fair.

One Thursday towards Christmas it nearly happened. She parked the baby near the gardening tools; he was asleep, buried inside his all-in-one snowsuit. Louise had a Ladybird book that Father Christmas had given her that morning at playschool. She couldn't read but she loved books. She sat down crosslegged on the carpet at the foot of the pushchair: she knew what to do by now, and that Mummy was going for a wander and would be back soon. But Sarah felt flat. William was nowhere to be seen. She had picked up his absence before she put the brake on, but it had become automatic, and there was still the dog food to buy. She was disappointed; this was Thomas's last lesson of the term, and the shopping would have to be done by car next week – there was simply too much to carry at Christmas. Emptily she picked her way through the shop, glancing here and there, staring at goods rather than at pictures in her mind. At the pet-food counter she bought more dog food than usual and tucked it in her shopping bag. She craned her neck to check that Louise and the baby were still all right, and then drifted deeper into the shop, towards the gloves and scarves and plastic macs. From the rack on the end wall she picked up some gloves, unboxed and separated as if another customer had been interested in them, and tried them on. They were pale leather, lined with something warm and natural. Beautifully made. The sort that would last for years, except that she always lost gloves, so they would be wasted on her. Her husband said she ought to keep hers on elastic, like a child. He had got tired of retrieving soggy remains off the drive where she tipped them from her lap as she got out of the car. The drawer in the hall was full of half pairs, talismans to ensure their partners were never found. She inspected her hands in the expensive leather, turning them this way and that, admiring them.

Off to her right the staff door in the end wall opened. She knew it was William without turning. He didn't walk straight through. Out of the corner of her eye she saw he was carrying something, a cardboard box. He put it down on the floor, only a matter of yards away, and squatted beside it, tossing packages onto the racks. She gazed at her hands again, glad she had something to do, to keep her there. She pretended she hadn't seen him. There was a maker's label hanging from one of the gloves and she carefully tucked it inside, to imagine they were really hers. She practised using them, touching things with them, to fill in the time. He had finished unpacking the box but for some reason hadn't moved; something was holding him. In her mind's eye she saw his face turned towards her; he was concentrating on her, she could sense it. Another customer passed by and he didn't move, didn't break his gaze. She felt extraordinarily confident, female, watched. She knew she had given him no sign, sent him no messages, but she was receiving something, she was sure of it. She allowed herself a tiny glimpse sideways, and then glanced the other way, so he shouldn't think she had been looking round to see him. Again she pretended she hadn't seen him. But she had been right. He was staring at her, very seriously, very beautifully. He looked even more beautiful now, still and serious, than when he was laughing and bestowing gifts.

She felt slightly breathless. This is real, she thought, nothing I have created. Dizzily she moved a little way down the racks, testing him. She sensed him shift position, following her progress. She stopped in front of the golfing umbrellas and reached out to touch one with her expensive gloved hand. They looked right on her, she thought fleetingly, perhaps she wouldn't lose these. William rose to his feet behind her. She was aware of him standing, looking at her. Through her elation she thought helplessly: what do I do if he comes over to speak to me? What will I say? She heard his footsteps; he was walking towards her. I'm satisfied with very little, she thought joyfully, this will keep me happy for the holidays.

There was a cry. From the far end of the shop, a baby's cry. The footsteps stopped. Louise's voice: 'Mummy!' Everything was grinding to a halt. Damn it, she thought savagely. Damn it, she thought, as she ripped off the gloves and rushed back to replace them on the shelf. She saw William's head twist away, a half-smile on his lips, a misjudgement made. He wasn't interested in mothers. He wasn't going to say anything to her now.

She slammed back to Louise and the baby, furious. The baby's face was red and blotchy. She hated it. It looked so ugly, spoiling her afternoon. She unstrapped it and picked it up, feeling lumpish and motherly, despising her crooning words. There was nothing wrong, just the waking grumps. She looked from the baby to Louise, despairing. They devoured her. She felt close to tears. I'm never alone, she thought miserably, never. I wouldn't be so silly if I could be really me. She was angry, cross with herself for caring so much, and blaming them.

The trip to the supermarket wasn't treat time today. Louise wanted to push the trolley, but wasn't strong enough and refused to admit it. The trolley kept turning in circles – they had picked one with a left-hand list and it was too late to exchange it. Even she had difficulties with it; she had to say 'Sorry' and 'I beg your pardon' more than once, seething inside. The supermarket had chosen this particular time, just when everything was busying up for Christmas, to alter its entire layout. She kept missing things, getting in a muddle, it all took twice as long. When she thought she had finally finished she checked through her list and found she had forgotten the salt. She had no idea where salt was, she couldn't remember seeing it, but she couldn't manage without salt. She caught a flying assistant, almost grabbed hold of her, to stop her escaping. 'Far wall,' said the girl, pointing over to the other side of the store, acres away, and pushed on. The trolley was laden; she couldn't face manoeuvering it all that way back. 'You wait here,' she said to Thomas. 'Right here. Look after Louise and the baby. I won't be a tick. I've got to get some salt.' She glanced around and thought, soft drinks and sweets, reminding herself where to find them again.

Thomas was like his father, very sensible. He said, 'OK Mum,' importantly. He liked being left in charge. He never did silly things.

She hurried back to get the salt, weaving her way through the crowds. Why did everyone walk so slowly, why didn't they look where they were going? She couldn't find the salt at first. There were boxes of Christmas crackers everywhere, puddings, tins of party biscuits. This didn't look like a place to find salt. She had to ask another assistant. She had been looking in the wrong direction. She turned her back on the Christmas specials and there it was. She grabbed a tub and fought her way back.

She had gone beyond sweets and soft drinks before she realized it; she must have missed the children. Two ladies boxed her in with their trolleys, nattering, as if this were a social occasion, not an ordeal. She was rougher than she intended with one of their trolleys and had to smile apologetically and say, 'Sorry,' again. Still she couldn't find the children. She pulled herself together and looked carefully at the aisle. Sweets and soft drinks. Perhaps there were two of them. They all looked the same, that was the trouble. There was a trolley near her, unattended. She suddenly realized it was hers; her shopping bags hung from the hook at the back. There was no baby in it. No Thomas beside it. No Louise dancing round it.

Frowning, containing herself, she checked the two adjoining aisles. There was no sign of them. She could think of no explanation. Thomas must be holding the baby; the pushchair was the other side of the checkouts. Why would he want to lift the baby out and take it somewhere? She smothered a flickering picture of someone else lifting the baby out, someone else with the children. No one stole three children, the idea was ludicrous. Or was it? If you wanted one, would you start with three, to sound convincing? But Thomas was sensible. She had told him, hundreds of times. Surely he wouldn't? She didn't know what to think.

People were rushing by, busy, uncaring. She imagined herself, vulnerable and pathetic, unable to keep her voice normal, saying: 'My children have gone. I left them here, only for a moment – it was only for a moment, I promise – and they've gone.' She couldn't think what to do. She couldn't act when she couldn't understand. She didn't want to move away from the sweets and soft drinks; they might come back, magically reapppear. But suppose they had become muddled, lost, like she had? Suppose they were waiting, hidden by the racks, only a few yards away?

She leant on the trolley, staring into it, as if it might contain some clue. Under her weight it moved, swung round in its irritating pendulous way. A hand reached out to steady it and a voice said, 'Life of their own, haven't they?' and then with a lift of recognition, 'Oh hello.'

She looked up. It was William. He was holding a large jar of coffee in one hand, no basket. She felt weak, disoriented. Her children were gone, and here was William. He smiled at her, beautifully. Someone was playing a hideous joke on her. For a moment she wondered if she were going mad, whether she had done it all by herself.

At last she said the only thing she could say. She said, 'My children have gone. I've lost them.'

William stopped and his smile disappeared. He looked serious. She told him, 'I left them here. I said not to move. The trolley's here but I can't find them. I don't know what to do.'

William glanced up and down the aisle. He asked, 'You mean the little girl and the baby?'

He knew her children. She was surprised. The way he said it, matter-of-factly, as if it were something he had always known. Images shifted at the back of her mind, turned themselves upside down, reinterpreted themselves. Gloves: she caught a glimpse of gloves, expensive, mortifying gloves, and intimations of some vast, ludicrous error.

There was no time to identify it now. 'Yes,' she said. 'And Thomas. He's eight. He's sensible. He wouldn't wander off. I know he wouldn't.' She heard her voice rising; she couldn't help it.

William said reassuringly, 'Well, they must be in here somewhere.'

She looked around despairingly. The place was busy and enormous. She didn't want to leave the aisle and the trolley, it was where they were meant to meet. If they were all wandering round she might never find them. She whispered, 'They know to come back here. I don't understand.'

William stared at her and then said practically, 'Go and look for them. I'll wait here. If they turn up I won't let them disappear again. Go on, it's better that way round.'

She frowned at him, wondering what he meant, and then saw a picture of three children, lost, being approached by a young man who said, 'Come with me, your mother's waiting,' and understood. How clever of him, almost as if he knew about parents and children.

It didn't occur to her to refuse, to be polite and say, 'Oh, I couldn't put you to that trouble.' She didn't even thank him. She nodded and turned to look for them.

As she walked she tried to think rationally, to plan a methodical route so she couldn't miss them, but her confusion got in the way, disorganizing her. And she had to look normal; she didn't want to appear like a silly mother, panicking over nothing. She saw someone she knew, a neighbour, and turned her back, refusing to be recognized. She couldn't face spreading the panic wider, not yet. She felt stupid, as well as confused. She walked faster; she didn't want to leave William waiting too long, he might give up and wander off, not understanding the importance. But she had to search properly. She slowed again. There was no point in rushing it, risking missing them; that would be even sillier.

But there was no sign of them. At last she approached the sweets and soft drinks again, dragging her thoughts together, ready to signal to him that she must check the far end, for him to hang on just a little longer, please. She was looking for his face, at adult height, and for a moment she thought he had gone. Then a customer moved out of the way and she saw him, by her trolley, with his back to her, squatting on his heels, doing up the dungaree straps of a little girl, a little girl who was Louise. The baby was in the trolley, and Thomas was standing beside William, their heads on a level. On unfamiliar legs she walked towards them. Thomas saw her first and ran to greet her, his face bursting with explanation.

She put on a smile and said, 'Goodness, where have you been? You *have* had me worried,' trying to sound light and ordinary. William's head glanced round, as he still adjusted the clips on the dungarees.

Thomas spoke insistently. 'I had to take her. You know what she's like. We couldn't see you anywhere. We went to the staff ones, like last time. She couldn't manage the straps, and I was holding the baby. I couldn't leave her. We came back as fast as we could.' He knew he hadn't done wrong. He had coped, all on his own. He knew he shouldn't leave the baby, so he had managed that as well. He moved closer and whispered, 'Louise says she knows him. She said it was all right to let him help.' He looked unsure, as if at the last he might have slipped up, made a small error. William was grinning. He gave a final tug on the loose end of the strap and rose to his feet.

She reassured Thomas, smiling at William over his head. 'Yes, it's all right. He was waiting here for you. He works at Jennings. We see him every week when you're with Mrs Simmons.' She spoke to William.

'Thank you so much. I do feel silly.' She should have thought of it; it seemed obvious now. She was a fool, all afternoon she had been a fool.

William shook his head. 'Don't. I know just what it's like. I lost mine once – Tracey – she's only three. In the market. Only for a couple of minutes, but it seemed like a lifetime. I was on the point of calling the police out. Mad panic.' He pulled a mock-chaotic face.

She stared at him, bemused. It had never occurred to her that he might be married, a father even. That he had a life all his own, was a family man. She suddenly relaxed.

William waved the coffee jar aloft. 'Well, I'd better be getting back. They'll think I've done a bunk.' He ruffled Louise's hair and the child gazed up at him, beaming. 'Bye-bye trouble. See you the next time you're in.'

She put her hands on the trolley, in control again. 'Come on kids, choose something quickly. We'll be late for Daddy's tea if we don't buck up. Goodbye.' She smiled briefly at William's farewell wave. She had even quite enjoyed saying 'Daddy' in front of him. Someone called *him* Daddy, she realized. She breathed out deeply. Goodness, she did feel better. As they pushed the trolley to the checkout she was smiling to herself. She joined the shortest queue, still way back into one of the aisles. But you had to expect queues at Christmas, they were just one of those things. She gave the baby the satsumas to play with. Her mind was quite clear now. She thought of gloves, and wanted to giggle. Nothing awful would have happened. He was nice; he would only have said something like, 'Can I help you?' It would have been a moment's embarrassment, nothing more; and mortification didn't exist when there was no one else to know it. She stretched out a hand and absently caressed her daughter's head. She might even call him William now, like the others, and not avoid him if it were busy, and not leave Louise and the baby stuck in a corner. There would be no point anymore. She sighed, still smiling, still stroking Louise's head. Never mind; she'd managed before, and nobody lasted forever. There was always the television.

THE HUSBAG

When Claire was a little girl, perhaps eight or nine, she had a dream she never forgot. It was a short and uncomplicated dream, or so she thought, a nightmare, and about, apparently, her mother.

In the dream she was standing outside the underground public lavatories at the municipal bus station – near where she lived at the time – waiting for her mother to emerge. She stood at the top of the steps leading down, watching; on either side of her towered the cast-iron railings surrounding the entrance, and above her the metal arch with the word 'Ladies' at its apex, in black letters on white enamel, spanned the descent. She must have been waiting some time, because she was anxious. The dream had started mid-wait, so she hadn't actually seen her mother go in, but she was down there, Claire knew.

After a while a figure appeared, walking up the white-tiled well towards her: a woman, but a faceless stranger, not her mother, a slightly larger woman, wearing a dark-coloured coat. Claire watched her ascend, and as she drew close, asked, 'Have you seen my mother?' The woman stopped on the steps in front of her, still not quite on pavement level, and replied, 'No.' Then there was a little pause, she raised her left arm showing Claire the object hanging from it, and added, 'But this is her handbag.'

At that point Claire woke up, terrified. The menace in the dream was unmistakeable and heightened, somehow, by the baffling incongruity of the woman's words. But she knew enough about handbags to appreciate that whatever else a woman might be prepared to lose, a woman and her handbag were rarely parted. She understood the private nature of handbags, a place where money and other things of importance were kept, a region children might not explore without permission. Something terrible must have happened to her mother, down there.

For years Claire saw the dream as a simple nightmare about the fear of mother loss. Since she could remember nothing about the domestic circumstances surrounding the dream she imagined – when she thought about it at all – that it must have occurred at a time when she expected separation from her mother: perhaps when her mother was going into hospital, as indeed had happened around that period; or before one of her own trips to stay with relatives in the country, a not unusual event in the school holidays.

But the dream must have been very powerful, because the images never faded. Over the years she told it many times to friends, when dreams were being discussed. It was a fine illustration of a classic childhood anxiety, she thought, and recounting it never failed to elicit a small frisson of remembered fear, as she smiled her way through it. Others apparently experienced something of the same, because it was always received with shuddering groans: it was a good, neat, horrific dream. Sometimes she improved it a little, making the woman's face change as she spoke, anticipating the menace, but this never became incorporated into the memory of the dream and always remained false: the woman's appearance, and her tone of voice as she spoke, had not in fact been menacing; only the words terrified.

Because the dream was so simple, and the significance seemed so obvious, it never occurred to Claire as she told it to think deeply about the details. She never wondered why it happened where it did, why she didn't enter the Ladies to look for her mother herself, why, indeed, she didn't even recognize the handbag.

But then she was deluded, because the facts needed to understand the dream were not available to her.

Claire's childhood had been happy, but not uneventful. When she was ten her parents had divorced. It was presented to the world as a civilized affair however, a mutual disenchantment, no rancour detectable. They were both teachers of progressive outlook, and although Claire didn't realize it at the time, the family environment was unorthodox for the fifties, almost avant-garde. It was very much in keeping for the divorce to be handled with tact and sophistication. Claire and her sister remained with their mother, but saw their father often, and accepted it as a mildly unfortunate fact of life. Four years later their mother married again, to a man the girls knew and liked, and who had the integrity not to interfere in their lives. Claire herself grew to adulthood through an exceptionally free and on the whole unrebellious adolescence, fell in love, married, and had children of her own. In her late twenties her father at last also remarried, to the relieved pleasure of all.

Thirty years after the dream, her mother died. Claire and her sister had loved their mother dearly; before the funeral they spent a few close days at the old family home, and in uncomplicated grief talked her life over, sharing their memories. Claire by now knew that there was no such thing as a civilized divorce; the two recalled their childhood, marvelling, not without pain, at the apparent equanimity of their mother's public face, when her first marriage must have been crumbling around her. Relatives and old friends called in to express their sorrow, new facets of their mother's life were unearthed, explored together, mulled over. The relatives and friends felt free to talk, assuming a

· knowledge among them that Claire and her sister did not in fact possess. Truths slipped out, incidentally. It had not been a mutual disenchantment, they discovered. Their mother had loved their father deeply, till the end. But for the last years of the marriage their father had been having an affair with another woman, a woman from his work, a stranger to the family. Despite knowing this, their mother had been desperate for the marriage not to fail. But it had, and although their father never married the other woman, their mother had lost.

Claire felt hurt, and upset that she had never known this. That her mother had been someone else as well as the mother she knew, a privately suffering woman, for a few years at least, and had kept that grief a secret from her children throughout her life.

Still, she comforted herself, it was all in the distant past, and her mother had recovered and remarried happily, and had probably done it for the best.

But then in the fragile weeks that followed, the pieces began to settle into place. Her mother's life was reassembled in her mind: the life of a woman now, not a mother. A woman, moreover, who in those privately turbulent years of her first marriage had been much the same age as herself, now.

And in the middle of one sleepless night she remembered the dream. She woke her husband and told it to him carefully, feeling on the brink of discovery. As she said it the meaning changed. Now she had the information, she couldn't understand how she had ever interpreted it otherwise. Suddenly she realized why it said, 'Ladies' above the entrance; why it took place underground; why, although she was female, she couldn't enter to find her mother, but remained where she had been left, an outsider above the hidden drama. She understood who the woman was, why she was faceless, and why the handbag wasn't recognizable, since it wasn't really a handbag at all. She understood the woman's words, they no longer seemed incongruous. And she reinterpreted her fear: fear of a mother's – family's – real loss now, not the imagined loss of a mother. Even the words 'handbag' and 'husband' were extraordinarily similar: only two letters different. That object of intimate importance, of security, the possession a woman was never easily parted from.

As she lay speechless on the pillows afterwards she knew she was right, with unshakeable certainty. The appropriateness of the symbolism seemed breathtaking; she admired her childhood mind, as one might a stranger's, for concocting it.

But most devastating of all was the realization that hit her minutes later, and reverberated in her mind for weeks afterwards: that although she had thought she had been unaware, all these years, she must, deep inside, have known.

BALLAD OF A DESPERATE MAN

When Graham was ten years old he lay in bed one night, fists screwed up into balls·against his chest, and prayed, desperately, that his parents would not divorce.

Four years later, reconciled to it, he begged again, into the darkness of the same room, that his mother would not remarry. The reasoning was unclear here; he knew only that he didn't want it, and feared it, and desperately hoped it wasn't going to happen.

Two years on, understandings reached with his stepfather, who was serious-minded and literary, so they had something in common, he urgently wished that Rosamund Bennett, eighteen years old and the most beautiful girl in the world, would fail to achieve the A levels expected of her and not go on to university, so he would get the chance to be noticed by her, and they could spend the rest of their lives together.

A year later, Rosamund a receding ache, he met Patricia. He didn't need to wish anything of Patricia; his desires, he discovered joyfully, were hers. He even half hoped he wouldn't get to university himself, so they could start their lives together, now. But he went, as did she the following year, and they married afterwards, undeflected by the wait.

Graham worked for the Civil Service in London. As a trainee, moving from section to section, he found the work interesting, but uninspiring. In his spare time he started to write, encouraged avidly by his stepfather, with whom he was now on excellent terms. He wrote reflective, dream-like prose, impressively atmospheric, he thought. Authorship excited him; he began to long, secretly but passionately, to see his name in print. He fantasized about recognition, even fame. Over a year he wrote eight short stories, investing desperate hopes in each, all disappointed. The pain shocked him.

Then came his move to Private Office. Suddenly work became intriguing, absorbing. He had no energy to spare now for writing, nor for mourning the fate of what he had written. He sighed briefly over the manuscripts, still dear to him, if not to others, and filed them away.

By thirty he was a Principal, comfortably settled near East Grinstead, close to Ashdown Forest. Patricia, still a vital part of him and successful herself in market research, detected hankerings. They decided to have a child. Patricia conceived easily, but was wretched from the start, and at four months began to bleed. Graham left her restless and tearful in hospital overnight, and in the darkness of his Sussex home, his heart set now on fatherhood, prayed fervently for the child to survive.

By the morning his wife was quiet, but empty. Graham was bitter, and recognized for the first time the failure of fate to provide anything he desperately wanted. But he comforted his wife, and there were consolations. The fault was in the baby, the doctors guessed. Though privately Graham doubted it, the loss might just have been a blessing, grotesquely disguised. And there was no reason why they shouldn't have another, as quickly as they liked.

So Patricia became pregnant again. This time she claimed all was well, insisted she could feel it, so confidently she convinced Graham too. He occasionally said to himself, 'I hope this baby's all right,' but didn't find himself praying for it. Patricia was so zestful, so obviously thriving. A perfect child was born to them, Judith. And four years later, because Patricia hankered again, a son, Richard.

For ten years Graham and Patricia were, in a routine, busy, unacknowledged way, happy. Early on Graham was promoted to Assistant Secretary, young enough not to have had to anxiously hope for it, and Patricia, always innovative, retrained as a computer programmer and worked part time when Richard started school. Their daughter tried and delighted them: a vibrant, tempestuous child, an explosive, passionate adolescent. She hated, adored, gloried, bewailed – nothing by halves. Graham was entranced by her, astounded and gratified – when not infuriated – to have produced such a spectacular child. Richard grew up sweet-natured, a quiet uncomplicated boy, predictable and undemanding. Graham loved him too, but peaceably, knowing it without being forced to realize it, as if the boy, like his wife, were part of himself.

When he was forty-five his department reviewed its needs, deplored its costs, and for the processing divisions – Graham's included – proposed a move. Only thirty miles, but northwards, the wrong direction, an impossible journey. Graham was alarmed. He was happy in his Sussex home: grandparents were nearby, Judith was less than two years from O-levels, at an enthusiastic, well-behaved comprehensive, Patricia's job was local, and important to her, and they would lose the Forest, which belonged to the family now. But proposals became plans, within six months. His apprehension grew; he began to wish, urgently, for insuperable obstacles, or implacable opposition. When the decision was finalized he was resentful, since he hadn't desperately wanted anything for so long, and still was to be denied.

He expressed his anger to his wife. Over the really important things, he complained bitterly, he never got what he wanted. You couldn't choose what to desperately want, they just were, and it was unfair, that they were always beyond his reach. He muttered peevishly about transfers, even, if it came to it, resignation.

Patricia, a sensible woman, chided him and reorganized the arguments. These things took time, she reminded him; they would still be here for Judith's exams, only months away now, and she could try a sixth-form college next, freer than school. For herself, well, computers were everywhere these days, a change wouldn't hurt. And there would be less travelling for him, more time to possess new forests, to enjoy a new, more beautiful home. Look at it, she urged, as an adventure.

Graham let his wife's positiveness soothe him and when the time came, helped her find the beautiful home. Judith raged at leaving her friends, but recovered instantly, and made new ones. Patricia found a computing job, better paid than the last. And Richard shrugged off the upheaval, still co-operative and undemanding, and no trouble at all.

So Graham settled into his greenfield site, rehabilitated his empire, tried to see it as an improvement. He never again mentioned his anger at being denied what he most ardently desired. He still knew it was true, that it was his destiny to be deprived, in this small area, but could see it sounded churlish, when he had so much and others, increasingly now, had so little. A neighbour two lush gardens away was made redundant and had to sell up. The newspapers pontificated on urban decay, squalor, unemployment. Television roamed desolate Welsh valleys, bleak Northern wastelands. Graham obediently counted blessings, not disappointments.

Four years later, her son now sixteen, his nature disguised with truculent styles, and her daughter twenty, rampant at university, Patricia found a lump in her breast. Life moved, suddenly, at appalling speed. Graham didn't have time to desperately want anything. Examination revealed more lumps. Patricia had a biopsy, and was booked to have both breasts removed, within a week. Judith dashed home and treated them to wicked hysteria, then magnificent strength. Graham, befuddled with shock, could take neither, and was relieved to see her go again. The night before Patricia's operation he heard a thump upstairs and found his son kneeling on the floor of his bedroom, paralysed with misery. 'I don't like what they're going to do to her,' the boy gasped, clutching at his stricken body, 'I'm frightened.'

Graham didn't like it either, and was terrified, but knew his duty. He knelt beside his son and explained that this was how they were going to save her life, that she was strong and wanted to live, and that they must be strong too, like her. He wasn't afraid to show tenderness to the boy; he held him and stifled his anguish, along with his own, with words. But he was surprised by his son's prostration, and his depth of need. It made him realize how rarely he had had to be of use to him, how little, over the years, unlike Judith, the boy had asked of him.

Patricia came through surgery well. Richard had to sit his O-levels while she was still in hospital, but everybody was understanding; he was promised a place for A-levels anyway, told not to worry. Things began, in appearance, to improve. Patricia came home, undefeated. The boy's results in August were moderately good; although frail and tender from radiotherapy, Patricia celebrated with the rest of them. The winter seemed too long for her, but she brightened in the spring. In June Judith achieved a glorious First. Graham detected a desperate hope, despite himself, that his wife·was recovered, and wasn't going to die.

In September Patricia's check-ups revealed further, massive invasions. Already thin, over the next six weeks she lost a stone. Graham didn't know how not to desperately wish her to live, to reprieve her. He prayed he might be spared his destiny this time, since this was different, and there could be no silver linings. Lives would be genuinely and literally ruined, unlike the other times, when perhaps fate had thought it knew better. He clung to obscure hopes. When it became obvious she was dying there was too much to do to mourn, and his wife was too admirable to inflict his suffering on her. She gave up the chemotherapy, so she could be herself, properly, for the end. He took time off work to share the brief weeks with her, and at Christmas she died. Judith, now living with her boyfriend in London, stayed on for ten days after the funeral and grieved, noisily and therapeutically, everywhere. The boy, ghostlike by day, invisible by night, demanded nothing. Graham had nothing to give.

He stumbled through the numbness, and began to grow angry. He found himself wishing, vindictively, for terrible things, or heart-rendingly, for the impossible. He longed for the grey-bearded surgeon, the monster who had mutilated his wife and given them pain and false hopes, to die, hideously. The man lived on of course, though Graham scanned the papers. He was enraged by the protection he was giving his enemy, by furiously wishing him dead. He craved, despairingly, another glimpse of his wife, whom because she had been so much part of him, he had never realized how much he loved. Memories tortured him: them at the top of Snowdon, windswept, victorious, Lords of the Universe; making love naked in her parents' unkempt garden, carefully and hysterically, among thistles and ants; the moment of Richard's birth, the easy one, her face melted instantly from impossible effort to radiance, the most beautiful, he thought now, he had ever seen her. He understood that these were the joys he yearned for, and had had, without recognizing them, and was now never to have again. He even thought that perhaps he had killed her, that this was his punishment, for so desperately wanting the wrong things.

After five months the anger began to defeat him: he could see no end to it. He went to work, coped, came home, ate the meal his boy prepared for him, watched television or read until he thought he was tired, then went upstairs, past the silent room where his son studied, and raged sleeplessly in his empty bed. At weekends he cooked and kept house for the boy, unless Judith descended; he was amazed, when she was there, how he could talk and smile and spar with her, while the anger festered on beneath, corroding his heart. She congratulated him on his recovery, but confided that she was worried about Richard, so quiet and sad, and with exams so near. Graham wished himself quiet and sad; he envied the boy his peace, which apparently allowed him to study, every night, while he was being devoured and exhausted with rage.

A week after one of Judith's visits, he decided that what he really wanted to do was die. He brooded on it a couple of days, until he was honestly, profoundly sure of it, and then waited for Friday, when his son would be out all night at a pre-exam party, bullied into it by his best friend. The boy rarely went out these days, if it meant leaving his father in the house alone. He was reluctant when the night came and asked, 'Will you be all right Dad?' anxiously, as if seeking an excuse not to go. To Graham, Richard now looked painfully like his wife; he recalled how once the boy had been part of him, as she had been, before she was stolen from him. He wondered if having once been part of him, his son could read his thoughts: he shut his mind tight, and sent the boy away.

Between nine and ten he drank half a bottle of whiskey, and reaffirmed that he wanted to die. Then went outside, past the slatted double doors that hid his own car, and made his way down the drive to the free-standing concrete garage, its windowless bulk shrouded in vines and passionflowers. Inside, squeezed in amongst garden clutter, was his wife's car, L-plated, and now his son's.

He entered the garage and manoeuvred the up-and-over door shut from inside, straining at the handle over the car bonnet. Then opened the car doors as wide as he could in such confined space, and checked the fuel level, by switching the ignition on and watching the needle rise.

He climbed into the driver's seat properly, and twisted the key. The engine whined and turned over, but failed to fire. Frowning, suspecting he had flooded it, he waited a moment, then slapped the gear stick about, pumped the pedals, and tried again.

Shockingly, the car leapt forwards, crunching into the garage door. He gasped, 'Jesus Christ!', slammed at the gear stick, and after a steadying breath twisted the key again. The engine groaned, then heaved, then died.

Cursing fate, and the boy, for the state of the car, which meant he would now have to rig piping to the other car, or die slowly, in the big garage, he climbed out and rolled the car backwards to get at the buckled door. The horizontal locking bar was warped and obstinate. Exasperated, he forced the handle into reluctant movement; and it came away in his hand. He gave a howl of frustration and flung it through the air behind him. It hit the naked light bulb hanging over the roof of the car, shattering it. Blackness descended.

Graham knew garages were dangerous places, that there must be other ways. He wriggled round the front of the car, groping at the wall for instruments of death. He kicked something rubbery and solid, a coiled hosepipe, but could envisage no way, without a car, of killing himself with a hosepipe; nor with a rake, nor a mower, nor a tumbling pile of flower pots, most of them smashed now. At the back of the car he rammed his shin into hard metal. He kicked out at it and whatever it was fell forwards onto his foot. He heaved it off – an old gearbox – and reached out over the work bench for the back shelves, fumbling for tubs and bottles and jars. Several fell and bounced away, or smashed. Something smelt evil, after it smashed, but was lost now. He tore at a cardboard packet – slug pellets – put some in his mouth and revolted, spat them out again.

He gave up the jars and felt his way to the other side wall. His outflung hand grasped rope, looped from a nail, but there were no beams. He began to weep, and trying to steady himself found the bowsaw; wetness sprang from his palm, but he doubted he would bleed to death. Beside the saw was the axe. But it was too heavy to wield one-handed. Even if space had permitted a mortal blow, he couldn't have delivered it. He lurched on and smashed the windscreen of the car with it instead, which burst into useless granules.

Inside the house, distantly, the telephone rang. It went on so long he stopped and peered at the illuminated dial of his watch. He was too long-sighted to be sure, but thought it said 11.30: inconsiderately late for phone calls.

When the ringing ceased he stepped backwards, briefly disoriented, and struck his temple sharply against a protruding wall bracket, causing excruciating pain. He groped for the axe again and hurled it, with a cry of fury, across the garage. The noise was satisfying, so he did it, with lesser but still relieving effect, with the saw; then, since he guessed it would make a laborious and uncertain poison, with a five-litre can of engine oil.

He was suddenly overwhelmed with rage. In a frenzy he stumbled round the car, snatching at objects and hurling them into the blackness. They clanged on the car, thudded or smashed on the walls, a ricochetting hail of fury. He reached the door again, crunching windscreen granules underfoot, and shook the metal violently, adding the thunder. Then on to the hosepipe and pots, augmented now with fallen missiles, a bonanza of new and reusable ammunition.

The cut on his throwing hand tried to stiffen; pain stabbed. He blundered into one of the half-open back doors of the car, and knew he wanted to sit down. He felt his way inside, sweeping glass granules off the covers, and sagged onto the bench seat. Objects in the blackness around him scraped and clattered, finding final resting places. Then it was quiet.

A while later he was roused by a swishing, crunching noise outside. It passed by, close to the garage. He heard the metallic jangle of something being flung to the ground, his front door open, and bang shut. A whizzing, clicking, sound remained: the back wheel of his son's bicycle, spinning free.

After less than a minute he heard Richard's voice, very faint, calling him. He could imagine the voice travelling round the house, room to room, encountering silence. Suddenly it was louder, outside and frightened. It sped this way and that, growing frantic. Then the door rattled, joltingly. 'Oh Jesus, Oh God,' the voice moaned.

Graham knew he was being cruel, but couldn't reply. The boy struggled on with the damaged door, whimpering. It gave suddenly, and crashed upwards.

To Graham, used to blackness, it seemed momentarily bright, although it was only the weak spillage of outside lights, and the flash lamp in the boy's hand.

'Dad?' his son called tremulously, and flicked the beam across the wreckage.

'I'm here,' Graham said at last, knowing he couldn't let his son suffer any longer.

The boy made a choking sound. The beam searched the car. As it found him Graham lifted a hand to his eyes.

'Oh Jesus,' gasped the boy. 'What happened?' He started to move forwards into the garage, stumbling over the debris.

'I tried to kill myself,' Graham said, watching the clumsy movements behind the glare of the lamp. 'It didn't work.'

The boy fell over something at his feet and scrabbled at the side of the car to keep his balance. 'Please don't die,' he begged. 'I don't want you to die.'

'Careful,' warned Graham. 'I've made an awful mess.' As Richard came close he reached out and grabbed his shoulder, pulling him onto the seat beside him. The lamp slid to the floor of the car and extinguished.

'I thought you were dead,' sobbed the boy, searching with his arms for Graham's body. 'I was praying you weren't dead. Say you're not going to die. I couldn't bear it if you died too.'

Graham held his shaking, weeping son, his quiet undemanding boy, part of himself, as his wife had been, and after a while found he was weeping too: streams of grief, and love, and shame, not rage. He stroked the tears from his son's sweet neck, and felt the boy's arms, tight and imploring, around him. And in the darkness was grateful, tiredly, to be what the boy so desperately, needfully, wanted.

NOT IN SO MANY WORDS

Julian lowered his breakfast cup of coffee deliberately to the grass.

'I told young Tyler,' he said, watching his wife's concentrated expression carefully, 'That Robert belongs to the Wham-Bam-Thank-You-Ma'am school of literature.'

Sophie looked up from the Review pages of the *Observer*. 'Really Julian,' she frowned, 'You shouldn't inflict your prejudices on your junior lecturers.'

She returned her gaze to the paper. The downward tilt of her head caused iridescent hoops of titanium suspended from her ears to brush her jaw. Sophie wore her earrings exceptionally long, beneath hair exceptionally short. Because of her appearance she was presumed by Julian's more conservative acquaintances to have some connection with the performing arts. In fact she was a senior civil servant.

'He asked my opinion,' said Julian doggedly, Professor of Literature, with opinions worth soliciting. 'So I gave it.'

Sophie finished reading and folded the paper back on itself. She tapped the print below 'New Fiction' and held it out to him. 'Well,' she said, 'here's someone who doesn't agree with you.'

Julian took the paper ungraciously. It galled him that Robert's novels, though best-sellers and advertised vulgarly in the tabloids, should nevertheless still be reviewed in the quality press. His own fiction was discussed there of course, at length, but was unmentioned – and possibly unheard of – elsewhere.

His eyes skimmed the text, to get it over quickly. His delicate, normally agreeable features darkened.

'Powerful, virile prose!' he quoted angrily, 'Jesus!'

'Quite true,' said Sophie, who had been sent an advance copy by Martha, Robert's wife, for old times' sake. 'And you might add intelligent, exciting, and immensely satisfying. It's a rare talent, to write as well as he does, for everyone.'

'Really,' said Julian. He experienced a familiar ache in his lower abdomen. He pushed the paper away and creaked to a more comfortable, relaxed-looking attitude in the chair.

Sophie watched him, smiling. After a minute she said, 'And your writing, my dear, is beautiful, subtle, and profound.'

Julian glanced at her. 'And satisfying?'

'Of course. Really Julian . . .' She stood up with a short laugh, ' . . . you should see yourself. Do grow up. No one else would dream of comparing your work.' She stacked the breakfast plates briskly and turned for the house. 'And no one would guess,' she sighed, 'that he was once your best friend.'

'And the meek shall inhibit the earth,' Robert said scornfully a hundred miles away, and tossed the magazine he had been reading to the concrete. On the front cover, glaring up at him in orange print, Julian's story was trailered as 'Another Gem From Our Foremost Lyric Novelist'. Julian regularly wrote articles for the magazine too. Robert had never written a literary article, because he despised elitism. Also he had never been asked.

Martha flung her head back to finger dry her auburn hair, wet from a dip in the heated swimming pool. Her arms, raised above her head, were tanned and muscular. For the last eighteen months, since reaching forty, she had weight-trained weekly at a gym close to the London office of Third Degree (Market Research) Ltd, of which she was Director.

'Christ,' Robert complained, more forcefully, since she hadn't responded. 'If he's got something to say, why can't he just say it?' He leant forward and thrust his hand into his wife's face, thumb and forefinger a centimetre apart. 'You know why, don't you? Because what he's saying is so pathetically miniscule it has to be stuffed with verbiage to make it visible to the naked eye at all.'

Martha shooed the bulk of her husband away impatiently.

'That's outrageous,' she said. 'I thought it entrancing. And it's not what he says, it's the way he says it. Sheer poetry.'

'Poetry my arse,' snorted Robert. 'Self-indulgent crap. All words and no action.'

'It's a story,' said Martha wearily. 'He has to use words. You use them too, in case you hadn't noticed.'

Robert felt that his words, Powerful and Virile, somehow constituted action. 'You know what I'd like to do,' he said grimly. 'Score it down to its bones.' He grasped an imaginary pen and made savage, obliterating movements through the air. 'Right down. Then you'd see what a nothing it is.'

'And you'd be completely missing the point,' retorted Martha. 'Do stop this, it's so childish. You know perfectly well that Julian writes beautifully.'

'And I don't, I suppose?'

Martha made an exasperated noise. Robert folded his arms mulishly across his chest. He scraped his chair back and stared out over the pool.

'Of course you do,' sighed Martha, after a minute. She leant toward him. 'I adore your style. You know I do. It's passionate, honest, and stunning. And books have to entertain, to be read at all. Oh Christ . . . ' She pulled back suddenly. 'Why do I let you bully me into these ridiculous comparisons? Good God Robert, you haven't clapped eyes on the man for twenty years!'

Julian sat on the chesterfield at the inglenook end of the sitting-room, with Robert's unopened novel on his lap. He fingered the cover, shifting position to draw his crossed legs together more closely. 'It doesn't bite,' Sophie had hissed a moment ago, passing him on her way to the desk.

He opened the book and turned the title page.

'Who, or what . . .' he enquired, gazing at the credit for the quotation in the frontispiece, ' . . . is Meatloaf?' It was asked rhetorically. He assumed his wife wouldn't know, since he didn't.

'A rock singer,' replied Sophie, without lifting her head from the Equal Opportunity Commission papers she was reading. 'Simon's got some of his tapes.'

Julian disliked being made to feel out of touch with his son's generation.

'Not British, surely,' he said, frowning.

'No. American. Overblown and coarse.'

'Ah,' said Julian, relieved. Ignorance of the cultural output of America, he felt, could be legitimately forgiven.

'Clever lyrics,' said Sarah absently. 'And rather appropriate, I thought.'

'Doubtless,' said Julian, with some satisfaction, mostly provoked by the words 'overblown' and 'coarse'. Three of his own novels had been prefaced with quotations. Once Thomas Mann, once di Lampedusa, and once, daringly, Virginia Woolf. Robert, he was sure, had never employed a quotation before. He stared at it again, and suddenly saw himself mocked: a hideous, jeering, private joke.

He closed the book, regarded the cover fixedly, and looked up at his wife.

'How many deaths?'

Sophie glanced over her shoulder, frowning. 'Two . . . no three. Or more, if you count the air crash.'

'Jesus,' sighed Julian. 'And how many screws?'

'Oh Christ,' said Sophie irritably. 'I don't know. A few.'

'Any rapes?' enquired Julian. His characters rarely died, or made love, though they often thought about both, deeply.

'Oh shut up,' said Sophie, not looking up. 'You know Robert wouldn't write about rape.'

'I don't see why not,' said Julian bitchily, 'if he's so incredibly powerful and virile.'

'You're impossible,' snapped Sophie. 'If you want to read it, read it. If you don't, don't. I've got work to do. Christ . . .' she muttered, 'I wonder if Martha has to put up with this.'

'Ask her,' suggested Julian nastily. 'You'll be within shouting distance next month.'

'Will I?' said Sarah,'Oh yes.' She brightened at the prospect of four days in London, at a Civil Service expense hotel. She thought a moment. 'Right,' she said decisively, and reached for the address book.

'How'd you like to be sensitively caressed by Julian on a sunkissed beach to a backdrop of classical temples and applauding Greek Gods?' Robert asked Martha, a week after Sophie's letter had arrived.

'I beg your pardon?' she said.

'According to this woman,' said Robert, flapping the holiday-reading section of the Sunday paper at her, 'whose brain must be irredeemably addled, Julian's sensitive books will caress you on your sunkissed beach etc. etc. Bet she's one of his lecturers. Arse licker.'

'Don't be crude.' Martha was at the window, watching her eldest son manoeuvre a large motorbike up the hedged drive to the paddock. Robert's current novel featured motorbikes; he liked to use imagery that was clichéd, and even crass, and then confound the critics with a treatment that was convincing, and unarguably fresh. She wished he would finish the book quickly and dispose of the research material, before the boy was old enough to take it out on the roads and kill himself.

She turned to face her husband. 'I can easily imagine reading one of Julian's books on holiday,' she said. 'In fact I did, in Crete. Not everybody wants thrillers and blockbusters, you know.' She touched a finger to her lips. 'Caresses,' she mused, 'That's rather good. Yes. I can see exactly what she means.'

'Crap,' muttered Robert. 'And if you must meet Sophie, you can tell her I said that too.'

'We may well have other things to talk about besides your books,' said Martha evenly. 'But if the subject arises, I certainly will.'

'While I remember, did you read Robert's book?' asked Martha, returning to the hotel bar table with two last gin and tonics, the third night of Sophie's stay. Subjects exhaustively discussed earlier included the children, the ludicrous price of property in London and its environs, the frustrations of working for the EOC under an unsympathetic administration, and the uncreative and ultimately tedious preoccupations of market research in an election year.

'Terrific stuff,' nodded Sophie. 'I had a four-hour bath that afternoon. Simon read it too. I decided that if he must read about sex and violence he might as well have it from Robert, instead of some of the smutty hacks around. He's become quite an addict. And did you see Julian's story in the Review? It'll be in the collection they're bringing out at Christmas.'

'Brilliant,' said Martha emphatically. 'Made my spine tingle. Literally. I can't remember when that last happened. Quite beautiful.'

'Robert's books provoke occasional tingles too,' smiled Sophie, 'though I'm not sure they're in my spine.'

Martha laughed. 'You should see some of the fan mail he gets. Positively lewd. The publishers encourage it of course, with that ridiculous photo of him on the cover. Like some randy American beach bum.'

'I see they've plastered "powerful and virile" all over the paperback too,' said Sophie. She glanced at Martha and smiled. 'Julian was distinctly miffed.'

'Was he?' said Martha, smiling back. 'Well, you tell him Robert was enraged by that holiday reading review. The "sensitive and caressing" one.' She snorted. 'Amazing, isn't it, after all these years.'

They were silent a moment. Sophie sipped her drink, then lowered it to her lap slowly. She shook her head.

'We should never have done it, you know.'

Martha looked at her. 'What d'you mean?' she said indignantly. 'It wasn't our idea, if I remember rightly. Christ, they spent half the night and a fortune at the college bar persuading us.'

'I know,' said Sophie. 'But young men are so young.'

'And competitive,' said Martha. 'And arrogant.'

'Yes,' said Sophie. She sighed. 'Julian was so shocked, when I said I'd enjoyed myself.'

'So was Robert,' said Martha grimly. 'Quite appalled.'

Sophie drained her glass and placed it with finality on the table.

'Julian never mentions it, you know,' she said.

'No,' said Martha. 'Robert neither. She exchanged smiles with her old friend. 'Not in so many words.'

THE EXPERIMENT

Thursday 26 October

I shall start this diary where it all began, by saying that I have for years regarded myself as an unlucky person. Let me explain immediately that I am not suggesting by this that terrible things have happened to me, or that my life has been more than usually tragic, because it hasn't. I am divorced, it is true, but then so are a lot of women my age; the children didn't die cot deaths or fall victim to child molesters, and neither grew up to be a drug addict or homosexual, which these days probably counts as positively lucky. Jennifer is married and lives in Canada now, and perhaps it's a pity Geoffrey wasn't the adventurous one as we've never had much time for each other, but that has very little to do with luck. It's just one of the normal, mildly regrettable imperfections of ordinary life. No, what I mean by 'unlucky' refers quite simply to my extraordinary record where games, competitions, whatever, involving chance are concerned, and since this entry is intended as an explanatory preamble, I shall give brief examples.

First, my experiences with raffles. These are extremely numerous, as I have been buying raffle tickets – upwards of twenty a year – for the last thirty-five years. Yet I have never, even at informal, draw-on-the-night occasions, won a prize. Of course I realize that in most cases the chances are slight: the Christmas Pensioners' Draw, for instance, sells over

10,000 tickets and offers only twenty prizes, giving my five tickets only the slimmest of chances. All the same, I have been buying for years and whilst I know that the likelihood of winning in an individual draw cannot be enhanced by past failure, I nevertheless believe the law governing probability to be a trifle rigid in this respect, particularly since I have discovered that of the ten of us in the office (I work for Bowdens, the plastic cutlery people) I am the *only one* who has never won anything. Given that I am the oldest by five years, and move in more raffle-infested circles than any of them, this has to be remarkable.

Second, from the past, my luck at Monopoly. (Ridiculously trivial I know, but still perfectly illustrating my point.) Years ago I used to play this game regularly with the children. It was however an accepted feature of play that any property on which I bought houses was henceforth landed on by no one except myself (unless I was in gaol and unable to collect rent) and that if I bought more than one hotel I would immediately be assessed for crippling repair bills and summarily bankrupted. In one game, I recall, I passed Go only once without forfeiting my two hundred pounds four spaces on in Income Tax. I am by nature an uncompetitive person and thus a good loser, especially with children; I seem to remember my fate upsetting them more than me, and the game is permanently associated in my memory with childish and genuinely pitying cries of 'Poor Mummy!'

And finally, very briefly, there is the office Grand National sweepstake. In this case I have simply dropped out altogether; again, not because I'm a poor loser, but because I like horses and couldn't take the responsibility. I chose a namesake horse once, Brave Vera I think it was called, and it had to be shot.

So, I have for some time thought of myself as unlucky, in this limited respect, but it was only a little over a year ago — soon after the first anniversary of my divorce, I remember — that I decided to stop merely thinking it, in some nebulous, unsubstantiated way, but actually to start recording evidence of it. This decision, I should add, was taken not in morbid spirit, far from it: I saw it rather as an entertaining diversion, and a welcome sign that I was emerging from mild depression following the divorce into a much more positive frame of mind. Because the fact is that I have always found numbers fascinating and figurework a joy; it has been one of life's minor disappointments, how little is actually needed to survive. Moreover besides a love of figures, I have some expertise with them, having worked for several years as secretary to the Statistician for the Area Health Authority. I borrowed extensively from his library and I think I could claim that by the time I left, when the Authority was abolished, I was at least as proficient statistically as he. (Where he had the edge was in his ability to communicate such concepts to the laity: I'm afraid I've never had that kind of patience.)

So it was with real enthusiasm that I began my 'luck' book, and in my eagerness to provide data for it I undoubtedly bought more raffle tickets, sent off more unsolicited Prize Draw Numbers, and participated in more office sweepstakes (excluding the National) than ever before. And it was when I reviewed the year's entries that the idea came to me, the idea that in development — which I'm coming to shortly — inspired this account. Because study of the pages of data, and acknowledgement of my inability to achieve any measure of success whatsoever, raised in my mind for the first time the possibility not just that I was unluckier than most people, but that this result was, in a statistical sense, *significant*. That is, I was contemplating for the first time the notion that my bad luck was NO ACCIDENT.

Now after the initial revelatory excitement a certain resistance to this idea crept in, simply because it didn't seem to lead anywhere sensible. I also made the mistake of mentioning it to some of the women at work, whose reactions reinforced my hesitance. They weren't willing, quite honestly, even to look at the figures, but were inclined to pooh-pooh the suggestion out of hand, and in one instance, actually find it terribly funny. So for quite a long time I fought against it, because no one likes to go out on a limb, intellectually speaking, and besides, even I could see difficulties in the idea. However I did continue to maintain my records, and so of course every so often the urge to tidy up the figures would come upon me, because there really is nothing messier than uncollated data; and then it came into my mind – in fact it was a conversation with Cheryl at work that provoked it – how generally *stupid* most other people are. I showed her a letter I had written to the Department of Employment criticizing their use of the Mean when calculating Average Wages Figures. In it I had pointed out that the Mean was a most misleading statistic to draw from a skewed distribution such as earnings, and only spread resentment among ordinary workers, most of whom could with jusitification claim that they didn't earn that much, since thanks to the distorting effect of the few very high earners, most of them wouldn't. Much better, I stressed, to use the *Median*; not only was it statistically sounder, but since it would be lower, and by definition half the work-force exactly would feel prosperous beside it, the political benefits would be enormous. Cheryl, however, had great difficulty grasping the difference between a mean and a median, and when I explained in words of one syllable, said, 'Oh, you mean like a plimsol line?'

It was at that moment, I'm sure, that I resolved to ignore what other people thought, and trust the figures. And just a small step from trusting them, to pursuing them. So we come, finally, to what all this has been leading up to; my decision to design an EXPERIMENT. After all, I have been telling myself, I could go on filling my notebook forever with data that may well suggest and support my theory, but is never going to be able to prove it. It's time to take the initiative. I haven't worked out the methodology yet, but I can't believe it beyond me, and I must say that I'm looking forward to the whole exercise enormously. A great intellectual weight has been lifted from me; it's so gloriously simple, just to let the facts decide. Indeed, if it doesn't sound ludicrously extravagant, I might almost say that in this project, anticipating the hours of planning I shall have to put into it, and the mathematical rewards I am bound to reap from it, that whatever the result, I have discovered some Purpose in Life again.

Wednesday 8 November

The Experiment is designed. As I suspected, it wasn't difficult, once I had identified the prerequisites of the exercise. These are:

1. It must be simple, and the results easily understood. There is no point proving something if no one grasps you have proved it.

2. It must provide definitive results. Obviously I can't predict what these will be, and dealing with probabilities means no absolutes, but the confidence levels must be as rock-solid as I can make them. This means overkill, in a statistical sense.

3. It must involve other people, who are strangers to me. The more the better, to discourage conspiracy charges.

4. There should be an element of actual gain or loss, so as to reproduce as faithfully as possible the real-life experience I am investigating. However, the gains/losses can be trivial, as they are in real life.

So, here is the plan. After work next Monday I shall drive up to the Broadlands estate, which appears well-lit and of course is highly respectable, so I am unlikely to get mugged, and knock on doors until I have found twenty volunteers to help me. (As long as they are unknown to me they don't have to be randomly selected, since this isn't a sample survey). I shall say that I am conducting research into probability and explain that over the next fortnight I would like to visit them a total of four times, for no more than a few minutes on each occasion, during which they will roll a die six times, after first making a written guess at the result. Then I will roll the die once, after likewise, in their presence, recording my guess. For any correct result they will win fifty pence, unless I guess right, which cancels their win. (This is the nearest I can get to a gain myself, since I can hardly ask them to reward me!) Fifty pence seems about the right level: just enough to tempt, without being ruinous for me. I have calculated that at the outside, assuming they're right one-sixth of the time and I'm not right at all (which even with the worst luck in the world is surely unlikely) I should lose no more than ten pounds an evening, forty pounds in total, which seems an eminently reasonable price for settling it once and for all. I shall take a tape recorder with me to record all our exchanges (unnecessary, but this is part of the overkill) and I shall ask the volunteers to witness the written records with their signatures as we go along. By the end each volunteer will have made twenty-four guesses, of which one would predict four would be right, and I will have made eighty, which with 'normal' luck one would expect thirteen to be right. Results deviating from these averages will have definite probabilities associated with them. No need to go into the mathematics of it now; suffice to say that if one of my volunteers made no correct guesses this would have a probability of $5/6 \times 5/6 \ldots$ twenty four times, which is 0.0125, or a chance of one in a hundred. Pretty unlikely, in fact.

So, it is designed, and although I'm nervous about Monday, it is an excited kind of nervousness and I'm still looking forward to it. This must be apparent to others, because Cheryl has accused me of being uncharacteristically chirpy (I'm sure I've never chirped in my life) and has demanded to know 'what I'm up to then?' There is a quite unwarranted degree of suspicion in her tone, and it seems to me that there is no satisfying some people.

Monday 13 November
I have just returned from my first visit to Broadlands and it has all gone remarkably well. I have made myself some Horlicks but even so I anticipate a late night; the adrenalin is running high.

The estate is really most attractive. The houses are detached and mature-looking, all mellow red brick, and turned at angles to each other along curving roads, creating a delightfully rural feel to the place. In fact the only straight section of carriageway is the access from the main road up to the estate; deliberate policy I should imagine, since it is surprisingly steep. There was a builders' skip on the tarmac half-way up, the only blot on an otherwise immaculate landscape, though even this has been positioned with obvious thoughtfulness, under a street lamp and well in to the kerb. All in all, the place glows with responsible citizenship.

I had no problem parking. All the houses have at least one garage, leaving the roads clear, and it took me only twenty-four housecalls to select twenty volunteers. Nobody was rude to me. One gutteral youth with the word 'Cocaine' inexplicably daubed across his tee-shirt said, 'Yeah' at me a few times, but then couldn't promise to be in regularly over the next fortnight so I dropped him, and at one house the door was opened by two young children who said Mummy was out but would be back soon. I was a little concerned for them, but the inside of the house looked monied and well cared-for (as to be honest did the children) so in the end I decided not to inform the authorities and merely let the woman next door know, who promised to check up on them later. The other two failures were empty houses. I would guess that twenty out of twenty-four is an exceptionally high success rate, and that the prospect of winning fifty pences, which I mentioned early on in my spiel, was a strongly positive point.

In the event I have lost seven pounds tonight. Two of the volunteers were right twice, ten right once, and eight wrong each time. Almost, I would imagine, a text book spread. On the other hand my results were fairly unusual, because I wasn't right once either, and of course I threw twenty times. Probability 0.026 or one in forty. (Unusual, but not extraordinarily unlikely.) In fact at the time it felt more like good luck than bad, considering the aim of the exercise, and I don't expect it to hold.

There should be no trouble with follow-ups. Human beings are born gamblers: most of them seemed to regard it as a treat, and only one woman asked any questions about the methodology of the Experiment. She wanted to know why it was being carried out like this when matters of probability must be solvable mathematically, so I played the dumb researcher and said well yes, but I only knew what I'd been told, and sometimes it was necessary that the people in the field weren't in full possession of all the details. Ah, she said knowingly, you mean a double blind. We had a most interesting conversation subsequently, and I hope the acquaintanceship deepens over the next fortnight, as she sounds just my sort of person.

So altogether a satisfying evening, but above all relieving, since the preparations have been a strain. I was very nervous about tonight — silly as it turned out — and I haven't been sleeping well. Also because I went to Broadlands straight from work and didn't want to leave my recorder and notebooks in the car I had to endure some mild banter in the office. I haven't confided the exact nature of the Experiment, but I did say that I was undertaking some private research, and Cheryl immediately piped up with 'Going to prove how everybody's out to get you?' which temporarily shook my faith in her stupidity. And with having to leave everything by the desk all day I couldn't forget about it. As with other semi-automatic activities typing is extraordinarily affected by nerves; I actually had to give up with carbons and use the photocopier for file copies instead.

Tuesday 14 November
No empirical results to record (next visit not till Friday) but I am making this entry after being struck by a philosophical, rather than mathematical, aspect to the matter. Indeed an aspect, now I come to

think of it, that harks back to a remark made to me months ago, at the time I foolishly aired my hypothesis in the office, and Cheryl said, 'So what on earth d'you think's so special about you?' What I am asking myself now, but hedging around, because I haven't yet followed it through, is WHAT IF I AM RIGHT? In fact the question is written in rather larger capitals in my mind. I shall press on with the Experiment, naturally, but I can see that I must apply myself to this, and that it was most remiss of me not to earlier, since in terms of investigative logic this surely should have come first. In the very first entry, I suddenly remember, I commented on the idea 'leading nowhere sensible'; and yet here I am, going there! And it is all very well saying 'let the facts decide', but ultimately, I have to ask myself, decide what? I have a horrid feeling that this oversight stems from reluctance, and that since the question has always existed, but merely remained unaddressed (or more accurately avoided) that I have been guilty of acting with two discrepant minds, one – dominant till now – which wants urgently to develop, pursue and prove a hypothesis; and the other, hitherto muted, which intuitively foresees, and has no desire to face up to, the consequences. This is not good enough. So I am going to make myself tackle it, despite sensing fairly momentous conclusions. I will report further, when they are clarified.

Thursday 16 November
Here is the further report. It is going to be difficult, so I will take it step by step.

First, let me say that I have just reread Tuesday's entry, and realize that the 'two minds' figure of speech showed extraordinary prescience. I am of course still one person, but I do feel that since I started exploring this question my mind has split into two operating modes: one firmly prosaic and practical and still keenly investigative (I have, for instance, just prepared report sheets for tomorrow with real, and almost innocent enthusiasm) and the other . . . well, rather overcome, to be honest, by the issues it has been grappling with. I understand much more fully now that earlier sense of reluctance, and I have to confess that merely entering this mode induces in me a muddle of conflicting emotions. It is as if I am being fragmented yet again: on one level there is a deep disturbance, almost an apprehension; yet on the other a tremendous excitement, and sense of awed anticipation. And this is without taking into account the natural inclination of mental revolt, produced by such a challenge to the rational brain. Because cutting the argument to its essence – and we might as well go straight there, though I dithered around it for hours yesterday before biting the bullet – to claim that one is significantly more unlucky than others is to suggest either that there is something special about oneself – and it would have to be very special indeed, to influence natural law – or . . . and I scarcely like to write it, though I must . . . that there is some purposeful force outside oneself – outside everyone, indeed – that has ordained one be treated so. I almost feel I should apologize for writing that, but I have thought about it all day, and I see no alternative. The very word 'significant' implies cause, or reason; if it cannot lie in other humans, and in this case it cannot, then it must lie in me, or in fate itself. And since I do not feel, and cannot believe that I am in any crucial sense different from my fellow man – certainly not on a scale capable of distorting the laws of probability – then if my hypothesis proves correct it is with fate, i.e. the purposeful force, that I am left.

At that point I have rather stuck. It has been effort enough, frankly, committing it to paper. My only solace, I suppose, is that I would appear to be falling into good religious company, though that would come better from someone who hadn't always claimed to be a non-believer. And even if I do suspend disbelief and entertain it, it raises nothing but questions. Why, for instance, should this purposeful force, God, whatever you like to call it, be behaving like this? What is the point? One could almost accept a divine bolt from the blue, in appropriate circumstances, but mischief at Monopoly? And if there is no point, and it is hard to see how there could be, why be so petty, and childishly malicious? And why, above all, to me? There, I've said it, and of course that's it, I felt the hurt as I wrote it. In heaven's name, why me?

But then again – and even as I contemplate it I sense the upsurge taking over – if I succeed, just think what I will have proved! In my head I hear a voice, tremulously excited. 'Have faith,' it urges, 'Go on, don't back away now, DO IT!' Gracious, I can scarcely grip the pen! Just think! It would be momentous, cataclysmic! An irrefutable, scientific proof! Surely, I tell myself – and the voice agrees, so enticingly – what the whole world has waited for!

That was foolish to write. Extremely foolish. I am letting excitement run away with me. Anyone would think it already proved. Also speculation along these lines sounds mad, whatever the logic. I think that for the present I should concentrate on the Experiment, and on preparing my results as professionally as possible. If it comes to a point where I want to share it with the world, well, the figures will say it for me, and others can draw their own conclusions.

I wish, rather, that I had not made myself tackle this at all.

Friday 17 November

Just the facts tonight and no speculations. I am too tired for more anyway.

I found all the volunteers in for this second visit. One old gentleman had actually delayed a social engagement for my sake and was rewarded by winning a pound. I have lost nine pounds fifty altogether tonight. He was right twice, seventeen were right once, and two wrong every time, though both were winners on Monday. There is an increasing tendency for volunteers to stick to the same number for their guesses, in the intuitive (though erroneous) belief that this improves their chances, and the six is by far the most popularly chosen. I had to decline seven cups of tea (all from winners, which may say something encouraging about the human psyche) but regretfully wasn't offered one where I had hoped for it, because she had to dash off to her Soroptimists' meeting. She seems on second acquaintance a very practical, busy sort of person, and made me feel slightly tired. Though I didn't call on her until towards the end, and twenty housecalls takes nearly three hours, so perhaps it was just me.

As far as my results are concerned I wasn't right once; but I'm not going to calculate the probability of this, or say anything more about it. I still have forty throws to go.

I hope I am not sickening for something. I do not recall feeling so weary after the first visit, and just writing this short report has left me quite exhausted.

Monday 20 November
I have now made three visits. I know I said I was going to leave calculations till the end, but I can't. I don't know how to describe the intensity of emotion gripping me at the moment, which makes my hand tremble even as I attempt to write this, but an approximation would be to say that I am appalled. Some coalescing process between states of mind has been creeping up on me for days, but only unified, stark and terrifying, tonight. Because I have now made sixty guesses on the roll of a die, in the presence of impartial witnesses, and I have not been right once. The volunteers have made only eighteen guesses so far, but everybody has been right at least twice. The probability of my result, no wins out of sixty, I have just calculated as 0.0000174, or less than one in 50,000. There scarcely seems point in continuing, though I suppose I must. Absolute certainty may not exist where probabilities are concerned, but I think I have come near enough, and that is why I am recording the result now, because whatever happens, it is proof.

This evening was a terrible ordeal. The tension I experienced preparing for my throws was almost disabling. Two of the volunteers asked me if I was all right, and I had to invent a story about drinking too much coffee before I came out to explain why my hands were shaking so violently. I haven't been in to work today and shan't again, till this is over. It is a horrible feeling, to be convinced beyond doubt that one has been deliberately singled out for bad luck. That one is, putting it bluntly, the object of divine spite. I feel on the edge of something terrible now, not something tremendous. I cling to the hope that when I publish, or otherwise get these results into expert hands, someone will be able to suggest a different explanation, but I fear they won't.

And I am haunted by new questions. Desperate, thought-numbing questions. Why, I keep asking myself, if I am able to prove what I have so easily — and it has been easy, ludicrously so, in the scale of things — hasn't anyone done it before? If this is a divine game, I cannot be the first to be so played with — God, I can't — and if I, a humble, only moderately educated woman with no previous interest in theological certainties can devise an experiment that conclusively proves what I have, then why haven't others? Or if they have, why don't we know about them? And if they truly haven't, why in heaven's name has this force, God, what you will, let me do it? That is the crux. WHY HAS HE LET ME DO IT? If he has the power to spite, he has the power to choose not to spite, surely? Does he suddenly want to be exposed? I can't believe it, not after all this time. Does he for some unthinkable reason place spiting me above protecting himself? Or does he simply not realize what I have done? Is he — most dreadful thought — not just a childish, malicious God, but a stupid one too?

There are no answers, and I am frightening myself.

Tuesday 5 December
Nurse Frinton says it's a miracle I survived. It doesn't feel much like a

miracle to me, attached to all these tubes and equipment, but little Nurse Rose claims it's impossible to look at anything positively with a catheter inserted, and assures me I'll feel quite different next week, when it comes out.

I don't remember anything about the accident. I recall the drive to the estate, and the evening's housecalls, but nothing at all about the drive home. They tell me the car hit the skip at more than forty miles an hour, and that a male passer-by, happily ignorant of every emergency First Aid rule, dragged me bodily from the car and several yards down the pavement, thereby saving me from certain incineration when the petrol tank exploded. Apparently this occurred with such force that several objects in the boot, including parts of my tape recorder, were found imbedded in the wooden wall of a garden shed twenty yards away. All other contents of the car, mostly paper of course, were destroyed in the subsequent conflagration.

The police have examined the remains for evidence of mechanical failure and found both the brakes and steering in their words 'severely defective'. However, and here I quote more extensively, 'while failure in both could have been present before collision, and thus been a cause of it, it was equally likely that they were in fact a result of it, since the impact had been considerable'. The 'equally likely' is I think a kind understatement on their part, as I received the impression from the Inspector who visited me that he thought the chances of a simultaneous brake and steering failure at the one spot in my journey where the result would be catastrophic, unlikely in the extreme, and although he was too polite to say so, that I had, for reasons unspecified, deliberately rammed the skip.

I suspect Cheryl thinks this too; she has visited with one of the other secretaries nearly every day, and it would explain her ingratiating and apologetic manner. All these visitors from Bowdens' seem to consider it their duty to pop in and assure me that my work has been taken in hand, so I'm Not to Worry About It (as if, in my condition, I would) and it was a great relief when Jennifer finally got her flight sorted out and I could tell them not to bother as my daughter would be here every day. (I have hazy memories of Geoffrey visiting, in the early days, but now he knows I'm not going to die he has confined his sympathies to letters.) Jennifer arrived a week ago, and apart from the pleasure of seeing her it has meant that I have at last got my personal possessions at the hospital, such as, thank goodness, my night-dress and towels, and of course this notebook. (Regarding this, and in passing only, I should say that both the police and my own doctor have apparently read it, though Jennifer, I think mercifully, has not.)

Really there is little else to say. I'm already strong enough to write, and now Jennifer is here they're talking about discharging me within a fortnight. I think, even with the catheter removed, I will still be dubious about Nurse Frinton's 'miracle' (it seems somehow entirely the wrong word but I believe I know enough about misfortune to recognize when I have indeed been lucky, and the folly of pushing it.

Cautiously, I would say only that the questions I asked in the previous entry have in my own mind been answered; and on that note of restraint I therefore close this diary.

THE SECRET

I'd had another row with Gerald at breakfast. About my work, of course, it's become almost a ritual. He said that if they were only filming for three days then I could come back every night, and I snapped no I couldn't, what did he think they were paying for, certainly not to shoot some motorway-jaded hag, and the argument went downhill from there. At one point he called me a pea-brained harlot (even his vocabulary is prehistoric) and at another I told him he had all the initiative and charisma of a telephone answering machine. Eventually he roared off to work half an hour late in the Audi, leaving me to take my rage out on the housework.

And that's when it happened. I had just got as far as the mantelpiece over my beautiful brass fireplace when suddenly I rose, effortlessly, into the air. 'It's the updraught!' was all that went through my mind, in the brief second before my head brushed the ceiling. I would have been alarmed, I'm sure, if the sensation hadn't been so exquisite. To describe it I can think of only one other as acutely pleasurable, and in a way this was better, because I was still capable of full and rational thought.

I didn't actually do much up there at first. I was still holding the duster, and I suppose I should have taken the opportunity to clear a few cobwebs, or dust the picture rail (sorry, I'm being facetious, it's the mood I'm in) but the fact is that I was so astonished, and then so delighted, that I did little more than swivel to regard the room – most odd from this aspect, almost like a cut-away film set – and relish the experience. Especially when I noticed the strips of old floral wallpaper that Gerald had missed when he painted the room last year, sprouting upwards like lurid fungal growth from the curtain pelmets. He's always so insufferably superior about my DIY efforts.

I floated around the room a while, not very elegantly – finding my wings, you could say, though in practice it was more like swimming, except less strenuous, air being so much lighter – and eventually managed a swoop through the doorway into the kitchen. The cat was sleeping next to the fruit bowl on the table, where she knows she's not allowed, so I dropped the duster on her from a great height, which made her look upwards in terror, and then shoot like a thing demented out through the cat flap; I'm afraid I laughed, feeling very childish and over-excited.

I was still drifting around the kitchen when I began to worry about getting down. Only for a moment however, because no sooner had the anxiety crystallized in my mind, than I sank, gently, to the floor. As if the thought had constituted a physical weight, making me just too heavy for flight. So I stopped worrying about it and rose again, this time to embark on an aerial inspection of the house. What struck me most, during this, was the profound effect of perspective: the furniture looked not only smaller, viewed from above, but in a strangely comforting way, much less significant. My dressing-table, his desk, our bed; all, suddenly, mere objects. I stayed aloft until afflicted by an attack of remorse, on hearing the rattle of the cat flap downstairs. You cruel woman, I thought, and dropped to the floor so fast I almost ended up in the linen basket. I ran down and found the poor animal still distinctly twitchy, but told her I was sorry and made a great fuss of her to prove it, and at least she isn't one to bear tedious grudges.

I didn't tell Gerald I could fly when he came home. Actually I didn't feel inclined to tell anyone, but particularly not him. Though fleetingly I entertained a delicious picture of myself lurking above the sitting-room doorway, perhaps repeating my performance with the cat, or making snidely authoritative remarks about his bald spot. But somehow I sensed it would be most unwise, and possibly, owing to the heaviness of spirit his presence invokes, even impossible. This was proved right; I tried a brief lift-off in the bathroom before I went to bed, and nothing happened. I put it down to the proximity of his soggy footprints on the bathmat, where he had stepped from the tub without bothering to dry any part of himself first. Sort of essence of Gerald, combining one of his most irritating habits with traces of his body fluids, enough to ground anyone. Paradoxically, the fact that I couldn't fly then tempted me to announce I could, just to see his reaction; somehow knowing I couldn't prove it made me feel safe. But by the time I entered the bedroom he was deep in his computing magazine, a choice of bedtime reading I find almost as offensive as if he were reading *Men Only*. (He sells office computers but won't have one in the house because he's terrified I'll crack it, and he'll have one less thing to sneer at me about.) So I was damned if I was going to say anything to him, despite knowing he does it deliberately to provoke this response. It's when he doesn't want sex, of course; that way he can blame me for it, rather than his own unreliable libido.

Funnily enough I didn't worry that I'd lost the ability to fly for good. Nor, which seems astonishing now, did I imagine that I might have dreamt it, or been temporarily insane. Somehow I knew it had been real, and would come back, when Gerald had gone. And it did; I watched his car pull out of the drive the next morning − yesterday − and simultaneously rose, as my spirits soared. I swooped up the stairwell, over the first-floor banister, and reckless with joy, dived head first down again, executing a satisfying twist at the bottom to avoid the hall dresser, and landing neatly on my feet in the middle of the carpet. I'm afraid no housework got done at all. Usually when I'm between jobs I virtually spring-clean the house, so the build-up of dirt doesn't offend Gerald too much on the days I'm working; but then usually I haven't got anything much better to do.

Carol rang me in the afternoon, to invite me over for lunch the next day. Today, that is. She'd just got back from Ibiza, where she's been modelling summer dresses for the Littlewoods catalogue. 'I can fly!' I wanted to shriek down the phone to her, but didn't. However I told her I'd got the part for the Marmite advert, which she whooped about, though really it's a bit of a come-down from the glamorous jet-setting types I used to land. But Carol's such a positive person, and always on the look out for silver linings you may not have spotted yourself. We can't go on being dazzling pouters for ever, she said, the sooner we move in on the family markets the better. Look at the OXO ladies, she reminded me, they roll in the bucks for years; and of course she's right.

Gerald was grouchy all yesterday evening, after I'd told him I was going to see Carol. He doesn't like her because she and Harry are divorced, and she's not as unhappy as Harry is about it. He thinks Harry got a raw deal, but since it was Harry's compulsive infidelity that caused the break-up, the logic is hard to follow. It has something to do with his belief that Carol was to blame for Harry's restlessness in the first place, and therefore should have been more understanding about the results; however I note the same arguments didn't apply when Carol started having affairs, even though hers were manifestly a desperate reaction to his. Despite the sour atmosphere, Gerald wanted sex when we went to bed, and I didn't have the energy to argue about it. He always wants to do it when he knows I'm going to be out visiting 'my' friends. I think he sees it as a stamp of ownership. While it was going on I decided I definitely didn't love him anymore, and infinitely preferred flying.

I left the Escort in the garage this morning, and took a taxi to Carol's; I knew we'd be drinking.

'My, you look wonderful!' she exclaimed, as she opened the door to me. Carol is very honest, insensitively so at times, so I took this as a genuine compliment. Truthfully I did feel rather wonderful. I take a lot of care with my appearance, because of my work, but I have noticed that over the last couple of days I've been able to take a lot less, and still be gratified by the results. I told Carol she looked wonderful too; though actually that's the wrong word. Now she's stopped starving herself down to a size ten, and accepted that natural tawny is much more attractive than bleached blonde, 'magnificent' describes her better.

We drank far too much Spanish brandy before lunch. (Not that it seemed too much at the time, but I can feel now it must have been.) Carol told me she had slept with a Moroccan guitarist from a beach café, and that his body was so dark and beautiful she'd never sleep with an Englishman again. (I doubt this, knowing Carol, but I'm sure she believes it now.) I told her things weren't any better between Gerald and myself, but perhaps without my usual note of bitterness, because she narrowed her eyes and accused me of being 'up to something'. 'You don't look at all miserable,' she said. 'In fact I'd say you look happy. Don't tell me you're not. What's going on?'

So I told her. I hadn't meant to, and I daresay the brandy helped, but I don't think it was just that. It suddenly seemed, well, all right.

Her reaction was odd. Not disbelieving, more wary. Perhaps she thinks I'm mad, I thought, it did sound mad. She asked me how I'd discovered I could fly, and when I could do it, and when I couldn't. All the right questions. And she asked me who else I had told.

'No one,' I said. 'Only you.'

'Not Gerald?'

'I didn't think I should. I didn't want to, anyway.'

'No one else?'

'No. Actually I wasn't going to tell you, but somehow . . .'
I smiled.

She looked relieved. She didn't follow it up immediately, but refilled my glass and then curled up in the armchair opposite looking extraordinarily satisfied and amused. 'I think,' she said with a chuckle, 'that the old dragon in the public library can fly.'

'What!' I cried, 'Not the one with the steel-wool hair and murderous glasses?'

'That's the one.' She gave me a sidelong smile. 'I had what I thought was a brainstorm when Harry left, and asked her for a book on women flyers. She showed me a book on Amy Johnson and I said that wasn't quite what I meant. So she dug me out a couple of novels. One of them was about a woman who has wings and is part of a circus, and the other was an American book that didn't actually mention flying at all, except in the title, but was about people being afraid of it. You had to read what it was really about between the lines. They came as an enormous relief.'

'You're telling me you can fly too!' The shock was followed by an upsurge of joy, and then a pang of hurt, that she'd never told me.

She smiled down at the brandy glass cradled in her lap. 'My mother could fly,' she said reminiscently. 'I remember her telling me once, when I was quite small. Of course I didn't believe her. It was the sort of crazy thing she was always saying.' She sighed, and looked up at me. 'Actually I couldn't fly in Spain, but I think I was too excited about my Moroccan. My spirit wasn't free enough. I haven't tried since I've been back, but yes . . .' she nodded at me, '. . . I can fly.'

'This is amazing,' I breathed weakly. 'But why on earth didn't you tell me?'

'You wouldn't have believed me, would you? Like I didn't believe my mother.'

'You could have shown me. I'd have had to believe it then.'

'Ah ha.' She tapped her nose. 'But I wouldn't have been able to. You can't fly in front of someone who doesn't believe you. Like you couldn't with Gerald. In fact I don't think you can fly if there's any risk of discovery at all. I thought I'd use it to paint the ceiling above the stairwell, but I couldn't until I'd bought the ladders. I didn't have to use them, but . . .'

'Hang on,' I interrupted. She was going too fast for me. 'Let me get this straight. What you're saying is that it's not just you and me . . . you're saying that lots of people can do it?'

'Well of course I don't know for sure . . .' she shrugged. 'But yes. In fact I think all women could. I mean that they're capable of it. In the right circumstances.'

'But not men?'

'My mother said they didn't need to. She said they could anyway, in a sense. I'm sure they can't do it literally. We'd all know about it, wouldn't we? You can't imagine them keeping it secret. They'd be boasting in the pub about how often they did it, or how high or fast they'd gone. And they'd have invented hundreds of rules to control it. And think of the warfare potential.'

'But . . . do they know women can do it? Some of them must. I mean . . . it seems incredible . . .'

'I sincerely hope not.' She laughed, then shook her head. 'I don't think so. My God, just imagine the anxiety, if they knew . . . we'd all live on tethers, or in cages.'

I digested this. At last I said seriously, 'But how is this possible? How can it be that women have the capacity for flight, and nobody except the women who have it know about it? That something so amazing could be kept secret, all this time?.

'Fairly easily, I'd have thought,' Carol said drily. 'From men, anyway. They haven't traditionally shown themselves riveted with interest in what women are capable of, have they? And even if they were told, and were listening properly at the time, they'd want to see it proved, wouldn't they? They wouldn't take our word for it. Christ, Harry wouldn't even believe me when I said I was upset, or something as simple as that. He'd say "no you're not" as if things that came out of my mouth had no connection with my inner feelings, and were either whims of the moment, or calculated tactics to oppress him. I wouldn't have stood a chance with "I can fly". Anyway, it'd hardly be in our interests to tell them, would it?'

'No,' I said. 'I suppose not.' I frowned. It was almost too much to absorb, on top of half a dozen brandies. A thought occurred to me. 'It's a shame it isn't more useful though,' I said slowly. 'I mean, if what you say is true, it's difficult to see how it could be used for anything except fun.'

'But that's just it!' cried Carol, 'Can't you see? That's its great virtue . . . it's ours, just for fun. Our glorious, unbelievable, female secret. What women have always needed. A totally frivolous self-serving talent. Marvellous.'

I nodded. Put that way, I suddenly saw it was. 'And I've learnt to fly because I'm breaking up with Gerald?' I said. 'That's it, isn't it?'

'I think so,' said Carol. 'Or rather, because of the way you're breaking up.' She paused. 'I only know four women who can fly. Mummy, the library dragon, you and me. That's not counting the two writers. Mummy was always her own woman, years before her time. Everybody thought she was wonderful, but completely dotty. Stacks of men friends, but never a husband in sight. She always said, "Men are such fun, darling, but not worth losing your wings for". I didn't understand, of course. The library dragon's a Miss, so she probably never married either, and she's so rude to everyone it's obvious she doesn't give a toss what they think of her. And me . . . well, the first time I flew was the day I accused Harry of having yet another affair, and he was so angry he punched me in the shoulder, really hard, and slammed out of the house. I felt so released, so completely free of him, that I simply soared up to the ceiling. I couldn't get down again till Elizabeth called round to weep over me about crashing her car. I felt dreadful, trying to be sympathetic and supportive, while my insides were practically wriggling out of my ears with excitement. She ended up asking me if I was all right, because I looked so pink and bothered.'

'But what about her?' I said eagerly. Elizabeth's a friend of ours. Widowed two years, the freest of us all. 'D'you think she can fly?'

'Oh no,' said Carol definitely. 'I'm sure she can't. She misses Hugh terribly. That's why she keeps crashing her car. And even when she gets over it . . . well . . . she had a good time with him, she'll want to do it again, don't you think? While you and I . . .' her lips twitched with amusement, 'well, quite frankly I prefer flying, don't you?'

'Even if you met someone like Hugh?'

She grinned. 'Well, I'm not saying I couldn't survive being grounded for a while. But permanently . . . no, not now I've experienced flying. It's too good to sacrifice for anyone.'

'It is good, isn't it,' I sighed.

'Wonderful,' agreed Carol.

I walked home. It's nearly two miles, and not the prettiest of city routes, but I was so elated, so brim-full of discovery, that I couldn't imagine cramming myself into a taxi.

And walking, I could look at the women. Near the main post office I saw one I was absolutely sure of, a beautiful woman in her forties, with eyes so alive and sparkling that I wanted to fling my arms around her, and a stride so bold and confident I guessed I'd end up in the gutter if I tried. I smiled at her as we passed, and after a flicker of surprise she grinned back. I expect she thought I was drunk; which I was of course, but I think I'd have smiled anyway. And I saw plenty of women who obviously couldn't, weighed down with shopping, and trailing children and responsibilities. Their faces, even when they looked kind and friendly, wearing that veil of care and selflessness. Like mine used to, I suppose, though I never recognized it.

When I got home – just a hour or so ago – I floated up and down the stairwell a few times, to check I could still do it and clear my head – gracious, it does feel good for you – and then rang Hogg and Sons, to tell them to start divorce proceedings. I was put through to Hogg Junior, who sounded very cautious; it's possible I was still panting a little from the exertion of the flight, and my cheerfulness may have struck him as odd, in the circumstances. He insisted he couldn't take instructions like that over the telephone, and said I should write, or call round in person.

I couldn't face another outing, so I picked up my pen to draft him a letter. But I wasn't really in the mood, and somehow found myself writing this, instead.

SUMMER STORM

The chalet had gaslights. And shiny satin counterpanes on the beds, a brass barometer in the hallway outside the kitchen, and four wooden steps from the verandah down to the pebble beach.

After we'd explored it we all stood on the verandah, overlooking the sea. Below us were two steep banks of pebbles, and then the breaking waves. Far out the sea was dark blue, but closer in, paler and yellowy.

'We'll be shipwrecked sailors,' Mummy said, 'abandoned on our desert island. We'll fish for our food, and live off the sea.'

Marie didn't like Mummy saying this, her face became twisted and unhappy. She said it wasn't an island and we hadn't been abandoned, and Mummy was stupid to say things like that.

Davey asked what were we going to catch when we'd only got nets, and there were no rock pools or sand, just pebbles.

'You wait till low tide,' Mummy said. She put her arm round Marie and jiggled her shoulders. 'Come on sweetie,' she said. 'This is a holiday, cheer up.'

We went for a walk along the beach track before we had supper. There was a whole row of chalets like ours, the people in the one next door had a red speed boat, pulled up onto the pebbles just above the sea.

Mummy said the grassy bank alongside the track was the sea wall.

There used to be a railwayline behind it, she said, but it was washed away ten years ago, when the sea broke through in a terrible winter storm. There were floods all along the coast, she said.

'Is that why the sea's called The Wash?' I asked. 'Because it washes things away?'

She said not really, it was called The Wash because it was so shallow, and washed in and out.

Davey said it wasn't fair, exciting things always happened ages ago, before he'd been born. Mummy laughed and said I hadn't been born either, not till the summer afterwards, and Marie'd only been three, and anyway there hadn't been any floods in London.

'What happened to the chalets?' Marie asked with a frown.

'They were all swept inland,' Mummy said. 'Way back, right over the railwayline.'

I think Marie was a bit frightened by this, but Davey and I weren't. When we got back from the walk we crawled into the dark space underneath the chalet. Above us it was just wood, painted with black tarry stuff, and the verandah at the front was propped up on concrete blocks. The chalet was a boat really. Davey said he hoped there was another huge storm.

Mummy lit the gaslights and we ate the corned beef hash we'd brought with us from London. Mummy said poo, weren't the gaslights smelly but I liked them: they hissed and made everything in the room look soft. Then we played racing demon, with four packs, and I won twice. Afterwards Marie asked if she could brush Mummy's hair, and Mummy said she was a big baby but she supposed so. She took all the pins out and let her hair fall down her back. Mummy has long black hair and when it was down she looked wild and young. Sometimes I wished my hair was like that instead of short, though mostly I didn't because then I couldn't pretend to be a boy.

While Marie was brushing Mummy's hair Davey went off and got the shiny red counterpane from his bed. He draped it over her shoulders and Marie spread her hair out over it.

'You look like a queen,' Davey said, 'and Marie and Claire are the princesses, and I'm the prince.'

I said, 'But I want to be a prince too,' and Mummy said of course I could be, I could be anything I liked.

Then Marie spoilt it by saying, 'I wish Daddy was here, he could be the king.' It was a silly thing to say, because Daddy wasn't there, and anyway he wasn't like a king, the way Mummy was like a queen. It made Mummy sigh and say it was long past our bedtimes.

In the morning the tide was out, and the sea looked more like an enormous lake. You had to cross miles of soft wet sand to reach it. Mummy said we could walk as far as we liked into the water, and we'd never be out of our depths. She sent us off with a big plastic bucket and the nets to find food. Marie didn't want to go, she wanted to stay with Mummy and go to the shop, but Mummy said if she didn't fish she wouldn't eat, and that was that. She told us to bring everything we caught back, and she'd tell us what was food and what wasn't.

There were millions of shrimps. So many the nets jumped with them as you lifted them out of the water. They were grey and see-through; you could see their stomachs like little black worms inside them. And there were small flat fish, about three inches long. We never saw them in the water, like the shrimps, they just appeared in the nets, and then tried to bury themselves in the sand at the bottom of the bucket.

We caught lots of crabs too. When we were a long way out, so the chalet was just a dot in the distance, Davey suddenly got the funny-horrors, and said crabs were biting his toes. He'd been scared by seeing the lobster pot, with a big black claw sticking out. We'd thrown shells at it and it had moved. He was laughing but frightened too, so Marie took the bucket and I gave him a piggyback all the way home.

Mummy said not to collect crabs unless we wanted to play with them, because they weren't the kind you could eat. The little fish were dabs, she said, they were fine, and so were the shrimps. She said we'd missed the cockles, which were the best of all, and showed us how to dig in the wet sand for them, fat round shells, just under the surface. She broke one open on the pebbles and ate it. We all screamed at her, because it must have been alive, but she just said yum yum in a gloating voice and did it again.

For lunch we had shrimp and cockle sandwiches. Everybody liked the cockles, except for a few gritty bits, and the shrimps too, though they took a long time to peel. Mummy ate the dabs, we didn't like the bones.

And that's what we did everyday, when the tide was low. Fishing's exciting, like hunting, and you never get tired of eating things you've caught. Anyway there wasn't much to do in the chalet. Davey decided the barometer must be broken. Mummy said you could tap it, gently, and it was the movement that was important, but every time Davey and I tapped it it stayed where it was, stuck on 'Fair'. Marie wanted it to go up to 'Fine', and Davey and I wanted it to go round to 'Stormy', so we could be swept away in our chalet-boat.

We swam at every high tide. Mummy let us change in the sitting room, so we could just run down the pebble banks into the sea. Davey got cold quickly because he was so thin, but Marie and I stayed in the water for hours. Marie seemed much more cheerful when she was swimming, almost like she'd been the last year, before she got so grown up and serious. I loved playing with Marie. I never minded it when she did things better than me, not like with Davey, when it made me angry and I had to try and beat him. Mummy didn't swim. She sometimes paddled at low tide, with her skirt tied in a knot at the front, but at high water she usually sat in a deck chair on the verandah watching us, and rubbing Davey warm. I think that's why Marie was so happy, because Mummy was close and she could see her all the time.

At supper on the fourth day Mummy told us that when we got back to London Daddy would have taken all his things and moved away to his new flat. Marie started to cry and Davey got cross with her; we all knew Daddy had a flat and even Marie had liked going up and down in the lift when we visited it, so really Mummy wasn't telling us anything new. She said we'd still see him at weekends and it was what they both wanted and it was nobody's fault. We only saw Daddy properly at weekends anyway, because he worked so late, so I couldn't see that it was going to make much difference. Davey and I went out to play after supper and agreed that Marie was being soppy. I felt a bit angry with her too by then; we'd played together all the time the year before and she'd become so different, and I hated the way she fussed around Mummy.

The next morning Davey caught an octopus. Mummy didn't believe us at first, till we showed it to her. It was about four inches long and transparent. She said it must be a jelly fish, but then looked closer and said goodness, it really was an octopus. It must be a baby, she said, washed up here by mistake. We were so interested in it that we left it too long in the bucket and it died, but Mummy said it would probably have died anyway, in such cold water, and we shouldn't be upset. We buried it in the pebbles under the chalet.

In the afternoon the needle on the barometer moved. It dropped to 'Changeable', though when we looked outside nothing much seemed to have changed. Mummy took us into Hunstanton on the bus and we had high tea in a café and bought postcards for Daddy. The lady who served us was surprised that none of us wanted fish with our chips. I chose sausages, Davey a pie, and Mummy and Marie had chicken. The chicken was very expensive but Mummy said she was treating Marie and we'd made our choices and she didn't want to hear any complaints. I liked it much better when Mummy fussed over Marie, rather than the other way round, so I kicked Davey when he whined about it.

Then after the chicken Marie didn't want to write her postcard.

Mummy said she must or Daddy would worry, and so would she. In the end she made it into a game. She numbered the postcards one, two and three, and Davey wrote on the first 'We cort an octapuss', then after Mummy had explained the game I wrote on the second, 'We did so too, Mummy didn't believe us either'. That made Marie smile, and although you could see she didn't really want to, she picked up the third and wrote, 'It had eight legs and a beak and Mummy says we must be the only children ever to have caught an octopus in England. Regretfully it died.' Mummy grinned over the postcards, especially Marie's, and said they'd make Daddy laugh, and we stamped and posted them.

When we got back to the chalet the barometer said, 'Rain'. It wasn't raining, but Mummy said that wasn't important and the needle had moved down very fast, and it did look as if we might get a storm. The sea was only half-way up the sand and the waves were still just ripples of foam, but it had got much windier, and the sky was dark yellow. Mummy looked pleased and said she liked a good storm, especially at the seaside, and if there was one we could stay up till high tide. Davey worked out that that would be at ten o'clock and bounced up and down shouting 'Can I really stay up till ten?' and Mummy said yes, just this once. Marie looked anxious and asked whether the water would reach the chalet. Mummy said no, it would just be a summer storm and they had lots of storms here, and she mustn't worry.

We started to hear the sea from indoors by seven o'clock. Davey and I went outside to look at it: the waves had got much bigger and curved over into green tunnels just before they broke. They'd reached the pebbles and were making them hiss. While we were outside the man from next door pulled his speed boat up the beach on wooden rollers and covered it with a grey tarpaulin. We helped him hold the ends down because it was flapping around so much in the wind. He said we were in for a real blow tonight. When we went in again Mummy had lit the gas lights and suddenly it looked very dark outside, and began to rain.

At eight o'clock we had Ovaltine and pieces of chocolate stuffed inside a long loaf. Marie kept jumping up every time the wind gusted and rattled the windows. Mummy said she must stop being a silly girl and such a worrier, and she'd never put us in danger, or anywhere she couldn't look after us.

Marie asked if she could brush Mummy's hair again and Mummy sighed and said why not.

She looked even more beautiful this time, because of the wind and rain and noise outside. Davey said there was electricity in her eyes. He asked if she would wear the counterpane again and she smiled and said only if everyone dressed up. So Davey ran round collecting all the counterpanes; I wore the yellow one, like a Roman toga, with my leather belt on top. Davey did the same, but he had to have his pinned up, to stop him tripping over it. Marie had the dark blue one and wore it over her hair, so she looked mysterious and foreign, like an Indian lady. Mummy wore the red one again and laughed at us, and while she was laughing a great gale of wind blew the verandah door open. We had to lock it to keep it shut.

Davey ran to the barometer and said it read 'Stormy' now, and Mummy grinned and said any fool could tell that. She held her hand up and said: just listen.

We all listened, standing there in our counterpanes, and the sea was a great roar in the darkness outside, louder even than the wind and rain. Davey wanted to go out onto the verandah to see it, but Mummy said not until high tide, because we'd get so wet, and we must wait for the right moment. But the rain kept hitting the windows and Marie cried that it was waves, and we were being swept away, so Mummy opened the window and shone the flash lamp outside, to show her how far away the sea was, and calm her down.

We sang car songs then, ones about the sea, Admiral Benbow, and William Taylor. Davey looked so funny in his counterpane that I kept laughing instead of singing, and he pretended to get cross but really he was showing off.

Then it was ten o'clock and Mummy said it was time to go outside. She unlocked the verandah door and it burst open on its own and sent a great gale of wind round the room. The counterpanes blew out behind us and made a tremendous flapping noise.

Mummy called, 'Are you ready?' with her hair flying behind her above the counterpane. She gave Davey the flash lamp and took me and Marie by the hand.

Outside it was hard to breathe at first. The wind was like a wall, you had to push yourself against it, and turn your face to one side to get air. The rain seemed to be coming from the sea, not the sky, and when Davey shone the lamp into the blackness it looked like white rods, shooting towards us. You could see the breaking waves even without the torch, and the noise of the pebbles being sucked down the beach was so loud it hurt your ears. Some of the rain wasn't rain at all, it was the sea, you could taste it.

Marie cried that the sea was too close, and she didn't like it. Every time a wave humped up ready to break she sobbed, and said it would reach us. Mummy shouted that no wave could reach us, and that this was the worst the storm would get, and look, we were fine. She made us stand in a row and said we had to shout, that that was how you showed you weren't afraid, and that storms were for shouting into.

Davey gave a little yell, and I did too, to see what it sounded like. Mummy cried, 'Louder, louder!' and I saw Davey's chest swell so I took a big breath too and we both yelled as loud as we could.

I heard Mummy cry, 'Marie, you shout too, shout the storm away.'

I thought Marie wasn't going to, she was half-turned away and shaking her head, but Mummy was yelling too now, and suddenly I heard Marie's voice, a great loud voice, loudest of all, screaming, as if the sea was the enemy. I couldn't believe she could make so much noise.

It made us all shout louder, and then we were all shouting together, like we were one person and part of the storm and everything in the world seemed to be made of noise. I could feel Mummy's hand holding me very tightly, sort of squeezing a message to me, and it made me reach for Davey's hand too. And holding onto Mummy and Davey I suddenly knew that we were doing this for Marie, and that Mummy had needed me to help her, and make Marie scream, and not be afraid. I was so proud that I was helping Mummy and Marie, and so happy in the storm, that I shouted and shouted and shouted, till my chest and throat hurt.

THE DUNGEONS

There were four trips down the dungeons a day, at 10.30, 11.30, 2.30 and 3.30. Visitors to the city castle paid extra for them, queued at the desk in the Great Hall for tickets, forty-five at a time. Unlike those at lesser castles – usually wishfully named, and indistinguishable from wine cellars – these dungeons were the real thing: for 300 years, from Tudor to Georgian days, the castle had served as the city prison. Now, though, it was a museum, displaying above ground the city's heritage, and below, its own, rich in ghoulish relics, and of indisputable tourist appeal.

Philip was guide for the 10.30 and 2.30 tours. A personable young man, it was generally held, with a good memory for detail – a talent much esteemed by the Curator, though in practice irrelevant – and a clear, attractive speaking voice. Philip liked the work. He liked the location, the responsibility and sense of leadership bestowed, and above all, the uniform he wore. Especially the short-wave radio at his breast, which could be relied on to crackle importantly at some point during the tour, and the bundle of keys at his waist, to which he had added several of his own, so as he walked they clanked and jangled impressively.

This Bank Holiday Monday the Great Hall was crowded by 10.15. Philip counted forty-five from the queue and apologized pleasantly to the rest. The visitors were mostly family groups: parents or grandparents with children, plus a few young couples. Among the group he noticed two women, in their middle thirties, one tall with straggling fair hair, the other smaller, moon-faced and plump. They caught his eye not because they were remarkable in themselves — indeed they were drably dressed, in greys and browns, and to his eyes plain — but simply because they were female, together, and otherwise alone.

At exactly 10.30 he unlocked the staff doors and led the party down two long flights of concrete steps to the dungeon door. He unlocked this too, threw the master light switch on the board outside, and stood back to let the visitors pass. They were entering the old guardroom, low-ceilinged and vaulted, where arrayed round the dusty brick walls were most of the surviving prison artefacts. The room was too small for the present inmates to circulate properly, a fact which occasionally inspired complaints: the official reply avoided economics, and stressed the educative parallel with its former use, along with a natural desire to please as many of the public as possible.

Philip closed the door behind him and turned to introduce himself. He liked to study the faces of the crowd at this point: some already lit with morbid fascination, some unobservantly neutral, and just a few — those who hadn't appreciated what they were paying to see — stiffening with shocked distaste. To all he offered an easy, welcoming smile.

His talk led him round the room in a clockwise direction. He moved swiftly from the tiers of wrist and belt shackles behind him — well-preserved and largely self-explanatory — on to the leg-irons, hanging from a large oak wall board. He explained that there were three weights of these, used according to category of offence and docility of the prisoner. As he spoke he slipped a hand behind the massive chain of the heaviest, swinging it imperceptibly from the board, and moving on, released it. A hollow boom made the crowd gasp and titter, and jerked the heads of the few not attending – among them the two women, on his left, reading printed broadsheets – towards him.

He moved on to the broadsheets himself now: copies of eighteenth-century posters listing offences and sentences, and in one case the published confession, extracted after torture, of a convicted murderer. He passed over them quickly; most of the crowd were too distant to make out the archaic script, and those that weren't soon bored of repetition.

On the opposite wall he pointed out the suspended shackles, a heavy yoke-like structure to which prisoners would have been clamped by wrists and neck before being hauled from the cell floor. Only a matter of inches, given the ceiling heights, but far enough for its agonizing purpose. Then came the wooden whipping post: he asked for a male volunteer here and was offered a burly young man pushed forward by his grinning girlfriend. Philip demonstrated how, with the young man's wrists positioned at right angles across the post, shoulder-high, his back was held flexed to its broadest and most vulnerable extent.

Lastly, in this room, came the scolds' bridles and ducking stool. Since his talk had so far been delivered in a jaunty, slightly gleeful tone, it was perfectly in keeping for him to term these 'his favourite'. This drew from the men – and a few women – familiar smiles and chuckles. He explained how the cast-iron bridles – more ovate cages really, bearing little resemblance to equine bridles – would have fitted around the woman's head, with the lock at the back and the palate flap forced over the tongue, so she couldn't talk, indeed, scarcely swallow.

He beckoned the burly young man's girlfriend onto the ducking stool. This was a popular move, even wryly appreciated by the young woman herself. He explained the mechanism and Catch 22 witchcraft rules, while she blushed at him under her fringe. Afterwards he offered her his arm to dismount, and rewarded her with a wide, expert smile.

Now he opened a heavy iron gate to the dungeons proper, and led the party through. On the left of the passageway was a square doorless chamber. This, he explained, had been the condemned cell. It was too small to accommodate everyone, so he waited in the passage while the crowd circulated through.

When they had regathered he asked if they had noticed the tiny peephole, high on one of the walls? Through this, because of the steep fall of the land outside, could be seen the castle gates, and in the past, the hanging gibbet. A warder would have kept watch through it, waiting for the signal to bring his prisoner up for execution. They might also have noticed the circular trap in the ceiling, a later Victorian addition, cut in the days when the dungeons were used to store coal. Sometimes, he told them, drunken young men prised up the manhole cover at night, and dropped in for a laugh. They didn't realize how dark it was down here, and that there was no way out, and had to be released by keepers in the morning. He made the experience sound spooky and chastening, preparing them for thrills to come.

They passed a barred mock-up cell next, with a life-size wax model of a shackled prisoner inside. Then a wire cage containing an iron gibbet, a scrap of skull bone still embedded on the central spike. On shelves around the gibbet were stacked plaster death's heads of convicted murderers, moulded from their corpses. When these were made phrenology was a serious science, Philip explained; if the shape of your head matched these you could be deemed criminal and incarcerated here, for no other crime than that.

The two women were standing beside him now. The lighting was poor in this area, draining their faces to a bloodless grey. Their expressions were grim. He smiled to himself, momentarily imagining them as authors of the other, rarer type of letter, complaining not of the tour organization, but – in vitriolic terms, using words like obscene and pornographic – of the morality of such a tour itself. Letters that made the Curator sigh with exasperation, as he despatched an 'exercise of choice' note in reply. Philip wondered what people like that expected, when they bought tickets to 'dungeons'.

He directed the crowd down a short flight of steps and entered the next room behind them. From the stairway he told them that in the central area, where most were gathered, had once been the stretching rack. There was immediate movement to the sides, as if the ghosts of agony should be respected. Then he pointed to the shackle pins round the dusty walls, where other tortured prisoners had been hung. The crowd swayed inwards again in confusion. There was really nowhere in the small room to go, and not stand in a place of suffering.

Now only a final cul-de-sac chamber remained, through the doorway opposite. He crossed the room to stand outside, and ushered everyone through. He let them mix and jostle and appreciate how crowded it was for forty-five, before telling them that up to sixty prisoners would have been locked in here. Without lamps, he added sepulchrally, in complete darkness.

The crowd barely heard him. He had dropped hints already; they were expectant, excited, whispering furtively among themselves.

He asked, smiling, if people who were afraid of the dark would now make their way back to the guardroom. A couple with young children squeezed past with apologetic grins and left. He scanned the remaining crowd. Most were turned to him; all, in fact, except the two women, who were leaning against the far wall, their faces only inches apart, talking earnestly.

Before he turned the lights off he warned everyone that the blackness would be absolute, that their eyes wouldn't get used to it, and that on no account must anyone strike a match. The mortar in the walls was crumbling and tinder dry; the authorities – he made his voice grave and ominous – would deal most severely with anyone endangering others with a naked flame. As a titter of laughter filtered across the crowd he threw the light switch.

In the darkness a hum of voices rose, restrained and where they were distinct, self-consciously normal-sounding. As usual he regretted the lack of a cell door. It would have added greatly to the effect, he thought, to have a heavy door slammed at this point, and for the crowd to hear a great key scrape in the lock. As it was he stood still and silent, to make them think he had gone. He counted slowly to 120.

When the two minutes were up he told them – through the darkness – about the mediums who refused to enter this room, and the numerous sightings of ghosts. He let oohs and aahs mingle with laughing groans, then lit his hand lamp. In the sweep of the beam the crowd blinked at him, looking herded and animal-like. He told them the tour was over and he would lead them back to the guardroom, but this time by torchlight, as prisoners would have been led out.

He retreated through the rack-room, swinging the torch behind him, and stood at the foot of the steps. Lurchingly the crowd followed. With an experienced eye he gauged who would require a steadying hand on the steps, and who could be left to grope. Most grinned at him as they passed, still sheepish and blinking. The two women were the last to leave. They neither grinned not groped, and following them back to the guardroom he heard their voices, still deep in whispered conversation. He caught up with them on the stairs outside and was about to say something, when the tall fair woman threw her head back and gave a harsh laugh. He disliked the sound, and felt an sudden, vengeful, flash of anger.

In the afternoon the castle was at its busiest. It wasn't until Philip was walking the queue, which was difficult to distinguish from the general throng, that he noticed the women again. They were in the line, ninth and tenth, so they must have started queuing early. He was surprised, and then, predominantly, pleased. He forgave them the laugh, and idly wondered if it were the dungeons, or himself, that they had returned to see.

In the guardroom they stood in front of the rusty shackles, directly facing him. He found it briefly disconcerting, to be speaking to faces who had heard the same words four hours ago; then realized they probably hadn't. The thought restored his confidence.

He lost sight of them beyond the leg-irons and didn't approach them again until he reached the scolds' bridles and ducking stool. At the words 'my favourite' two young men near the front guffawed, provoking squeals of outrage from their girlfriends. Through the chuckles of the crowd behind he was aware of the older womens' faces, intent and unsmiling, watching him.

He asked for a volunteer for the ducking stool and in sudden devilment, eyed the women directly. The small fat one stepped back hastily, into a family standing behind her. The fair woman grasped her arm, steadying her, and swung round to apologize. Philip let his gaze pass on quickly to the young couples, so quickly he was able to glance back at the kerfuffle the women had caused, and smile at it with the rest. He beckoned one of the squealing girls forward. Out of the corner of his eye he saw the two women threading their way back through the crowd. He helped the girl onto the stool, smiling at her broadly.

He missed the women in the confined gibbet and condemned-cell area, and only spotted them again as he descended the steps behind the crowd into the rack-room. They were the far side, huddled in the doorway to the final chamber. When he spoke of the rack and wall pins only they, and he, remained motionless. It annoyed him that they had so quickly found the only other untortured spot.

They stayed very close as the crowd filed into the last chamber. He wondered if they were going to leave before he turned the lights off, but this time when he offered the escape, no one took it.

He threw the switch. A quiet hubbub rose from the crowd. Philip heard it, but at a distance, across a pool of silence surrounding him. He knew the women were within it, breathing the same musty air, but as he counted, found himself disbelieving it. When he snapped the torch on he experienced a small shock, seeing their faces so close. He caught the tall woman's eye, and although he flicked his gaze away, was aware of hers still resting on him. As punishment he refused to light the steps for them on the way out; he heard whisperings as they ascended, but they didn't complain.

The next morning, the holiday over, the Great Hall was quiet. A knot of dungeon visitors – no need for a queue today – was collected loosely round the cash desk. At 10.15 Philip clanked across the flagstones. Twenty foot away he ran his eyes over the group and realized, with a jolt of surprise, that the two women were there again. In the same greys and browns, exactly as yesterday. Almost as if they wanted to be sure they were recognized.

He said, 'You again?' when he took their money, in a jocular tone, as if what they were doing might not be unusual.

'Oh yes,' nodded the taller woman, without returning the smile, and turned deliberately to her friend. Philip knew he had been rebuffed. Frowning over it, he took a £10 note from the man behind, and had to be reminded to give change.

Downstairs the women stood in front of him again. This time they were impossible to ignore.

He started to talk. But the words sounded different: somehow shrivelled, as if punctured by the women's presence. He lifted his tone, trying to inject more cheerfulness into it – and was alarmed to hear not cheerfulness, but triteness in his ears.

He moved on quickly to the broadsheets. But the party was so small the women could move with him; he could only avoid their eyes by not looking at anyone. He was forced to fix his attention on the objects behind him; and found the shift of focus itself disturbing. Phrases that had been chosen for people resounded oddly against iron and wood. On several occasions, especially at the ducking stool, and later, in the rack-room, he thought he detected an unpleasant undercurrent of reproach. He blamed the women for it, though he couldn't definitely locate the source. At the end, in the darkness, he found himself counting faster than usual, and had to make himself slow down. For the first time ever, he realized, he wanted the tour over.

Lunchtime he spent in the canteen with Paul, one of the security guards. A single young man like himself, they sometimes drank together after work. Philip thought of mentioning the women, just casually, but couldn't decide whether to pitch it as a genuine puzzle – perhaps even a security matter – or a joke, and in the end said nothing.

At 2 p.m. they walked back together to the Great Hall. From the arched entrance Philip could see the dungeon cash desk and leaning against it, reading leaflets, the two women. He said 'Shit!' under his breath, and then, 'Nothing,' with a shake of his head, to Paul. There wasn't time to explain; he wished now he had said something: he could imagine them laughing about it, or even, if Paul had taken it seriously, questioning them, together.

This time, as they bought their tickets, both women smiled at him. He refused to smile back. As they turned away he saw their eyes meet, and heard a soft laugh. He experienced a powerful desire to step forward and punch them, hard, for confusing him.

He led a party of twenty-eight downstairs. In the guardroom the women stood further back this time, in the middle of the group, but he was still aware of their gazes, steady and unsmiling now, locked on him. He turned sideways, blotting them out, and concentrated on the objects again.

He ran his eyes down the shackles and leg-irons. And at the bottom, he noticed something extraordinary. A few – not many, but more than one or two – were tiny, as if they had been fashioned for midgets, or children. He was astonished. He knew that children had been imprisoned here; it was incredible that he had never seen the evidence before.

Disoriented, he moved on to the broadsheets; and with his eyes fixed on the published confession, noticed – again for the first time – the dates. The calculation was easy: the tortured murderer, at the time of confession, had been sixteen.

He heard his voice continuing – asking jokily for a volunteer at the whipping post – while inside his mind whirled. He had reached the ducking stool before he could reconnect himself to the words. He was relieved to get out of the stark lights of the guardroom into the gloomy passageway, and collect his thoughts.

They passed the condemned cell, and then the shackled prisoner scene. At the wire cage containing the hanging gibbet he found the women very close, almost brushing his shoulder. He pointed to the bleached fragment embedded on the central spike, and in the instant of saying the word 'bone', saw it, horrifyingly, as bone himself. He could even visualize, from the curve of the fragment, the skull it had been part of.

The image of a pinioned skull stayed with him through the rack-room, and into the chamber beyond. In the darkness it intensified so vividly that twice, trying to shake free of it, he lost track of the count. Leading the crowd out at the end he wondered if he was sickening for something, and that was why he felt so strange.

Upstairs in the staff-room the feeling subsided. It came to him, as it drained away, that what he had experienced, although it had felt real at the time, had in fact been manufactured for him, by the two women. It had to have been; because nothing was different down there, nothing at all, except their persistent, inexplicable presence.

He set off to the canteen for a cup of tea, and on the way was struck by a sudden, revolutionizing thought. He turned on the spot and walked quickly back to the Great Hall. The middle-aged balding figure of the other guide, Fred, was already there, taking money from the 3.30 queue. Philip scanned it closely.

He hadn't realized how much he wanted the women to be there, until he saw they weren't. He wished almost, as he turned slowly away, that he hadn't checked.

That night, at home in his bedsit, he thought about the women, with frustration and anger, most of the evening. The dungeons too, though more vaguely, now just macabre backdrop to the womens' bizarre behaviour. It took him a long time to fall asleep, and when he did he dreamt chaotic dreams: of journeys, and missed connections, and lost documents, and luggage that disintegrated.

The next morning he woke unrested and walked to work through a fine drizzle. Before he mounted the steps to the castle he lifted his eyes to the hulk above, grey and near-windowless against the paler grey of the sky. As he looked at it, a trick of cloud and light made it appear to be falling, malevolently, towards him. He caught his crushed breath, tucked his head down, and hurried upwards.

At 10 a.m. he walked down the main staircase from the History of Transport Room to the Great Hall. From the half-way gallery his eyes found the dungeon desk. Behind it were a group of camera-slung Japanese, a dozen or so, and behind them, still in their greys and browns, the two women.

When the time came he took their money without comment. He thought he saw pity in their smiles, and felt his insides curl.

Descending the stairs he was aware, as never before, of a sense of oppressive depth. The vast weight of the castle above seemed to compress the air, making it heavy and thick. He turned the dungeon key slowly, and realized with shock, and then dismay at experiencing the shock, that he didn't want to enter. He swung the door open. The reek of stale human sweat hit him, even after a night of emptiness. He let the crowd assemble, closed the door, and started to talk, straining for a cheery note. The result, in his own ears, was grotesque. That the crowd failed to notice, laughing and entertained as usual, appalled him.

As he reached the scolds' bridles, his radio buzzed. He gasped 'Christ!' in confusion and the crowd thought it was funny, and laughed at him. His confusion turned to shaking fury. Beyond the guardroom gate he cut great chunks from his spiel, not caring if the women noticed, just to get it over, and in the blackness at the end regretted the lack of a machine-gun, rather than a door. On the way out he had to hold the torch in both hands, to steady its trembling beam.

In his lunch hour he sought Fred out. He was in the canteen, eating sausage and chips. Philip had no appetite; the unconsumed remains on Fred's plate looked to him revolting. He sat down in a chair opposite and told him he'd had two women visitors for the last five trips. He asked if Fred had noticed them.

'What do they look like laddie?' Fred asked.

Philip could see them in his mind, but found them hard to describe. 'One tall and one small. Brown and grey clothes. Thirties.' He shrugged. 'Kind of ordinary looking.'

Fred nodded sagely, and took another mouthful of sausage. 'Made an impression on you, I can tell. Hell boy, they could be anyone.' He gave a bubbling laugh through his mouthful, and said the only returner he'd had was a man caught later stealing shackles, who'd turned out to be a local pervert.

Philip said he didn't think the women were like that.

Fred leant towards him. 'It'll be you they're after laddie,' he hissed. 'Women that age . . . ah ha . . .' He waggled his eyebrows suggestively.

Philip found he had no breath to reply, but hoped his attempt at a grin was convincing.

Fred gave a mocking sigh. 'They'll be students, boy. Come all shapes and sizes these days.'

Phillip knew they weren't, but pretended to agree. On their way back to the staff room he nearly asked Fred to swop afternoon sessions, but then realized that after telling him, he couldn't.

For a moment, walking toward the queue at 2.15, he thought it was over. About thirty people were gathered by the desk, all strangers. He took their money quickly, his insides tense. He locked the cash box; and as he did so, two drab, familiar figures detached themselves from the shadow of a display board, and drifted toward him.

Philip unlocked the box again and took their money, without looking at them. He sensed them turn to join the group. Under his breath he hissed, 'Bitches, bitches,' to their backs.

Anger sustained him during the descent, and for a while restored a brutal jauntiness to his speech. But the effort was immense; even before they left the guardroom his voice was cracking with strain. He asked for no volunteer at the ducking stool, and led the party quickly into the gloom. Outside the condemned cell and the hanging gibbet he found he could half-close his eyes, unfocussing them, without anyone noticing. But at the entrance to the rack-room, with everything, the crowd, the women and the room, before him, he was forced to look, and could find nowhere to rest his gaze.

And then at the end, as he turned the lights off, the darkness played a terrible trick on him. In the moment light gave way to blackness the pale faces of the crowd appeared to rush, huge and threatening, towards him. The hallucination was so convincing that in the shock of it he forgot to start counting. When he remembered, he started immediately at fifty. His heart was still pounding at 120. He delivered his lines hastily and lit the torch. In its beam the faces of the crowd – even those of the two women – looked as tame and sheepish as usual. But the memory of what they had just been, and could at any moment become again, terrified him. Walking back to the rack-room steps he thought of dashing up them, leaving the crowd behind, to make his own escape first.

That evening he watched television in his bedsit until 2 a.m. He fell asleep in his clothes without turning the set off, and at intervals during the night was dragged back to consciousness by urgent voices, and jangling music.

In the morning he woke queasy. He changed his clothes and ate a small breakfast, but was overwhelmed by nausea on the stairs outside his bedsit, and vomited violently into the WC in the communal bathroom. Half an hour later he rang in sick, weak from muscle spasm and relief. He told himself, most of the day, that of course he was just ill, he had been sickening for something, all along.

The next day, Friday, was his day off. He visited his father at his garage the other side of the city, and took his father's two Dobermanns for a three hour walk by the river. At the back of his mind, all day, was the hope that finding him absent for so long, the women would give up.

Walking to work Saturday morning he was conscious of the castle's bulk, lowering over the city, long before he could see it. As he mounted the castle steps he kept his eyes downcast. He completed his duties in the History of Transport Room and at 10.15 walked down to the Great Hall.

Snaking back from the dungeon cash-desk was a long queue of visitors. His eyes travelled the line slowly, and saw only strangers. He walked down to the desk and sold forty-five tickets, a full tour. He was alarmed not to feel his heart lift.

He led the party downstairs. The door for a moment seemed unopenable; but he saw his hand, and the key, doing it, and drained of will, followed the crowd inside. As he turned to face them he finally acknowledged it: that what the women had summoned up lived on, without them. Reproach and outrage issued like suffocating smoke from the fabric of the dungeon itself. It billowed from the doorway behind him, gushed from the instruments of torture round the room, swirled round the features of the obscenely expectant crowd.

The acknowledgement bravened him. He made no attempt to humanize his words. He adopted a snappy, facetious tone, and when he came to the whipping post and ducking stool asked for volunteers as usual, blaming the vicious demands of the crowd for it, not himself. He spent longer than usual in the passageway, lingering outside the gibbet cage, insisting everyone had a chance to see. Though his heart swelled with the pain of it, until it felt it would burst. Beyond, in the rack-room, a mother smacked her misbehaving child: he wanted to kill the child, for crying in a place of torture; and then the others, for knowing it, unlike the child, and not crying. When he turned the lights off in the final chamber salt tears filled his eyes, and poured down his throat. He waited nearly four minutes before lighting the torch, in case even in the gloom, anyone should notice.

He ducked the afternoon session. He simply went home, without a word to anyone.

That night he got drunk. Alone, in a public house below the castle ramparts, on whisky and beer. He spoke to no one except the young barmaid, to order his drinks. He tried not to notice that she had tiny hands, and bony, childlike wrists.

At closing time he left the pub, lifted his face to the monstrous blackness above him, and stumbled towards the steps. He ascended, past the nightwatchman's dim-lit chalet, then the castle gate house, and across the dry-moat bridge. The huge castle doors, studded and battened, rose before him. He turned left, keeping in the shadow of the castle walls, till at his feet he found what he was looking for: the cast-iron manhole cover, over the condemned cell.

He knew the knack of lifting it, from replacing it in the past. How with fingers in the lever slots one edge could be lifted just high enough to ram the toe of a stout shoe beneath, to allow the heavy cover to be swivelled aside.

It shifted easily, with only a small metallic scrape. He sat down at the edge of the hole, swung his legs through, and dropped into the blackness.

It was further than he expected to the floor below. He landed joltingly on his feet, lost his balance with nothing in the blackness to fix on, and sat down heavily. For a moment he remained there, recovering himself. The world had reduced to a cold stone floor, the acrid scent of ancient lime mortar, and as his eyes accommodated to the darkness, the faint outline of the manhole above, grey and strangely solid-looking, like a dying moon in a starless sky.

He lurched to his feet and found he was too drunk to walk unsupported in total darkness. He groped for the wall and felt his way along the brickwork out of the cell. Then along the short length of passageway to the guardroom gate. At night it was kept closed, but unlocked. He turned the heavy handle, and swung it open.

The blackness swirled over him. He could smell it, thick and choking. He thought he could hear it too, pumping from the objects around the room; then realized it was his own blood, throbbing in his ears.

He felt to his right and rattled chain and wood: the suspended shackles, too robust to damage. Next, a smooth expanse of paper. A poster; he raised his hands to the top, and ripped it from the wall. Then a second, and a third. A bundle of leg-irons beyond unhooked easily, and crashed to the floor. The noise was gratifying; he repeated it with more leg irons, and then wrist shackles, till his ears rang.

He reached solid wood: the guardroom door. He turned and

blundered across the room. His hands met wood and shifting metal: the shelves bearing the scolds' bridles. He snatched one up, found bare wall, and squashed the bridle between the brick and his body, till the metal cracked.

Suddenly he wanted to urinate. He flung the bridle away and did it, swaying, in the direction of the whipping post. Fastening his jeans afterwards he lost his balance and staggered sideways into the ducking stool. A sharp prong of metal caught him painfully on the thigh. He wrenched at it, swearing savagely, and hurt his hand.

He was tired of the guardroom. He felt his way back to the open gate and set off down the passage. A few steps on his right elbow banged the cage containing the gibbet and death's heads. He slipped a hand through the bars and with a wild sweep of his arm sent invisible objects crashing and bouncing to the floor. He roared,'Yeah!', and rattled the bars in triumph.

He lurched on towards the rack-room. The passage curved; misjudging it, he caught the back of his injured hand on the rough brickwork of the wall. He snatched it to his chest, and lifted his other hand to steady himself. But the hand found nothing; he stumbled, trying to regain balance, and realized, too late, that he had reached the steps to the rack-room. He stepped down the first jarringly, missed his footing completely on the second, and fell forwards, into blackness. There was a rush of air, then a slapping thud, as his knees and forearms hit cold stone. He sank to the floor with a groan, and vomited where he lay.

Sometime in the night he woke and smelt death: the sour fumes of a tortured body, the innards ripped from it. The thought was passing and unfrightening, but the stench repellent. He rolled a little way from it and fell into unconsciousness again.

When the lights came on he woke and was briefly alarmed. He felt too ill to move and waited for the muffled shouts and clanking footsteps to find him.

The voices and hands were rough at first, then, as their owners recognized him, shocked and gentler. They lifted him to his feet.

'Bloody idiot!' old Fred hissed at him furiously. 'You're for the chop, laddie, that's for sure.'

'Christ man, what've you been playing at?' The other hands belonged to Paul. He sounded astonished, outraged. 'Boy,' he breathed, 'they're going to have your guts.'

Phillip swayed towards Fred, blinking. He took in the uniform, the radio, live and crackling at his breast, and the bunch of keys at his waist. He heard the words, and the anxiety and seriousness behind them, and suddenly laughed.

They led him out of the dungeons, an arm apiece, and along the castle corridors to the Curator's office. A young secretary, still in outdoor clothes, squeezed to the wall to let them pass. She stared at him with horrifed, excited eyes. Philip winked back at her, hugely amused.

The Curator demanded an explanation: the least he deserved, he said, after such an appalling breach of trust.

Philip knew there was one, but couldn't be bothered to try to say it. He said he'd done it for a laugh, because he was drunk.

The Curator, tight-faced with anger, called him a foolish young man and a great disappointment. He warned him that they would have to consider prosecution for the damage, and that as from now he should regard himself dismissed.

Philip grinned at him, light-hearted at the insignificance of it all. He leant over the desk for emphasis and said it was a stupid boring job anyway, and he didn't give a toss.

'I hope that's the drink talking,' the Curator muttered, and hastily called the guards back.

They escorted him to the castle gates. Below lay the city, still and sharp-drawn in the early-morning light. The view stretched for miles, high and wide, under a pale, airy sky.

At the top of the steps they released him. He descended alone, blinking and tottery, but euphoric and absolved; in his own mind now, and heart, a free man.

PAINTING PYLONS

I see the van as I near the stone railway viaduct, walking up the valley to visit a woman friend. Self-hire, back doors open, parked on the chippings track, where thirty years ago the steam trains ran. As I pass, a man in white overalls comes round the side. Howdo, he nods; 'Hello,' I say politely (we always talk to strangers here). I gaze at the paint pot in his hand, and then around: at the jutting lime kilns opposite, crumbling and bramble-choked; the vast quarries above, where before the great god Industry forsook the valley he bit voraciously into the mountain-side; and over the stone parapet into the gorge, down to the tops of ancient beech trees, their brilliant fresh-leaved canopies shrouding the tumbling stream beneath. I wonder what, out here, among ruins and the perfect decorations of nature, he is about to paint.

He trudges away from me, up the dusty sheep track beside the kilns. It's yellow paint, I can see it, splashed on the side of the pot. Then I look up, to the towering pylons, glinting gold to the waist in the sunshine. He's carrying a gallon pot of yellow paint, and he's off to paint the pylons.

They're huge, these pylons, to match the mountains. Steel legs braced to the slope, crossbars wide and hanging: great six-armed gunslingers, blasting power up the valley.

It's only a two minute dash to my friend's house.

'I've just met a man on the viaduct!' I pant excitedly, as the front door opens. 'He's off to paint the pylons!'

We hurry through the house to her cliff-edge garden. From here we can see everything: the mountains above, still in bare winter colours, grey and bracken-brown; below, the valley, a lush kaleidoscope of summer greens, rich, soft, and jumbled. With half-closed eyes you could leap into them, intoxicated, expecting to survive.

Across the gorge we can see the pylon clearly, and the one behind, both yellow-legged. No men on them yet.

'It's rust-proofing,' my friend murmurs, as we wait. 'They'll paint them grey later.'

'Imagine saying to your wife in the morning,' I sigh, 'Well, pylons today, see you for tea.'

The pylons rise from steep fields, the last before the quarries and mountain shale. Their feet are hidden from us, behind blossoming hawthorn scrub. At the top of the field there's another van, red, parked broadside to the slope. Sheep graze innocently nearby.

'There he is!' I shout. A tiny white figure has appeared, scaling the criss-crossed steel.

'There's another!' cries my friend, 'On the one behind!'

We're too far away to see their faces, but close enough to watch them climb: no ropes or harnesses, just white overalls, and arms and legs. The yellow stops halfway but they keep going; past the lower crossbar, and still climbing. From the top they'll be above the quarries, with the whole valley beneath them.

They've reached the top.

'Let's cheer!' I urge, clapping my hands. 'It's terrific!'

'They won't hear us,' says my friend. She grins at me. 'Let's take our clothes off.'

We laugh, and nearly do it. Alone, if I'd thought of it, I'd have done it. It would have been pleasant, standing naked in the May sunshine, offering my primitive salute. I'd never have known if they'd seen me, and afterwards I could have smiled over it, or forgotten it, as I chose.

A little later, as we laze in deckchairs, I reflect: it's nothing to paint. Slosh slap; I can paint. Everybody paints.

And pylons are ordinary. They're everywhere. Not pylons like ours, maybe, but even these, they're nothing special. We hardly notice them, or the power lines, except when they obscure a view, or sizzle in the damp.

The men aren't special either. Not really special. They can't be. They're men who can paint, and climb, and aren't afraid to look down.

But to paint pylons. To take your ordinary skill, apply it to a simple artefact, without fear, and become a hero.

I can paint, I think hopefully, as I walk home. Above me the pylons glitter, monuments in gold. I'm nothing special, but in my own way I can paint, splish splash.

And pylons are everywhere. They may look tall, but men straddle them, and I've got arms and legs too, so if they can do it, so could I.

I could even learn not to be frightened. It's only confidence; just say to yourself, you're doing all right, there's nothing to be scared of, you needn't look down. I could do that.

I'm home now. Our house is turned the wrong way: no gunslingers or gleaming monuments to be seen. Just me, and my life, facing a placid, unambitious hillside.

But I see a pylon. Right here, I see it. I thought I had dismantled it long ago, when I saw it as something else, esoteric and unscaleable; but I hadn't, it's still here, and it's just a pylon.

So my mind's made up. I know what I'm going to do.

Pick up my paint brush, look upwards, and start climbing.

I'm going to paint pylons.

THE SIEGE

Mary heard the sirens around 3.30 in the afternoon. Faintly at first, from the main road, then blaring and urgent-sounding, as the police cars entered the estate. She would have liked to go outside and see what was happening, but Geoff was watching television in the sitting-room and would be bound to hear the front door. He had been in a good mood today, and she didn't want to spoil it.

Louise knew something: her cheeks were puffing with excitement as she clattered up the back path at five o'clock.

'It's a siege,' she hissed, closing the door quietly behind her. She glanced over her mother's shoulder towards the sitting-room, wearing her sly, ready-to-be-dutiful look. 'Tony Wilmott's back,' she whispered. 'He got his divorce papers today. He and Sharon had a fight. He stabbed her in the arm and she ran out. He's in the house now, with the kids. He says he's going to kill them. There's policemen everywhere.' She unbuttoned her pink supermarket overall and tossed it onto the twin tub. 'I'm going over to Pete's. You can see it from his room. Tell Dad I'm at Janey's. Say we've got project work. It's college day tomorrow.'

Mary said feebly, 'But tea's ready.'

'I'll get something at Pete's.' Louise tweaked at her short bleached hair in the mirror behind the door. She hesitated, as if momentarily tempted to tackle the sitting room, but then snatched up her shoulder bag. 'Tara,' she said, without looking at her mother, and hurried out.

Mary ate her tea in the sitting-room with Geoff. She had cooked his favourite, chops, which meant hers had to be tiny; the vegetables were heaped around it to conceal its size. Paul had beefburgers in the kitchen. Mary had closed the door between the rooms, in case Geoff heard movement behind him and was disagreeably reminded of his son's presence. Mary wished the boy less disagreeable too, but for his own sake, and did what she could for him in small, unincriminating ways.

After tea Geoff went upstairs to get dressed for the pub, and Mary washed up. The boy, spike-haired and sullen-faced, sat at the kitchen table behind her, hunched over a comic. In another family, Mary thought, a mother might have said, 'Pass the plates dear,' or encouragingly, 'How about your homework?' As it was she said nothing. She wasn't even sure he had been to school. Before Geoff came down he would be gone again, for the safety of the streets. Mary knew nothing of her son's life; at fourteen he ate and slept here still, but had become a stranger.

The boy stood up. He was taller than her now, and heavier. He went to her handbag and rummaged for her purse.

'I'm taking a quid, OK.' It wasn't a question. Mary wouldn't be able to buy a television stamp this week now, but knew that if she couldn't protect him, she had to pay for it.

Once the house was empty she put a cardigan on and went outside. She liked to spend summer evenings in the garden, inhaling the free air. Usually she sat on the wooden bench that Geoff had made when they first moved here, in the days when he had been in work, and hadn't been so angry. It was cracked and lichen-scarred now, from years of neglect.

All around, crowded into the view above the fence, were cream houses with grey concrete-tiled roofs, identical to the one behind her, and within their walls people, barely a raised voice away. Sometimes she imagined the outsides of the houses stripped away, a doll's house estate, filled with model people, their lives lived in front of everybody. He may be ill, it made her think, but he wouldn't do it then.

Tonight she left the garden and walked towards the Wilmott's house. At the junction a police van was parked, skewed across the road, half-blocking it. Striped tape fluttered at waist height beyond. She couldn't see the house from here, only a knot of policemen further down, talking on the pavement.

She walked on, taking the long way home, round the block. She passed Janey's house, where Louise was supposed to be, and then young Pete's, where she was. She guessed Louise would stay the night, which would mean trouble between Pete and his father, again. She sighed at Louise's mischief, and pitied Pete, too young and eager to see he was being used. Beyond his house she crossed the road to avoid a group of boys jostling in the bus shelter, their bikes strewn thoughtlessly across the pavement. Through the dusk a blue light in the distance caught her eye, winked alarm, and disappeared down a side-street. There was no sign of Paul. She hoped he was being careful, with so many police about.

At home she made corned-beef sandwiches to leave on the side for Geoff when he got back from the pub. She glanced into the sitting-room to make sure everything was in its place, as he liked it, and then went upstairs and changed into her nightdress, but listening out, in case Paul returned before him and she had to go down again to tidy the kitchen. Geoff was very particular about neatness, especially when he had been drinking.

In the bathroom she washed her face and hands. As she folded the towel to replace it on the rail she saw in her mind's eye two tiny children, in the darkness of another house, watched over by a father with a knife. What is there to stop him? she thought, clutching the towel to her chest. How could Sharon do it, how dare she risk them like that? It made her breathless, to think of it.

She lay on the bed and pressed her head back into the pillow. Just a few more years, she told herself, not long now. Louise would go soon, she was clever; she'd use a boy like Pete, flatter him into taking her away. And Paul would be safe soon too, when he was big enough, and strong. Briefly the tiny children reappeared, their features clear: the girl impish and laughing, the boy just a baby, simple-faced, but sweet and trusting. She was filled, suddenly, with a terrible emptiness, and in a moment of panic wondered what she would be escaping for, with the children grown up, and ruined. But I did it for you, she imagined crying out to them, when they were all safe. Understand, love me now, it was for you. She realized she was weeping, and hastily wiped her eyes. Geoff was enraged by tears.

'You're meant to be at college,' said Mary fearfully, opening the back door to Louise at ten in the morning. She's gone already, she had told Geoff earlier, the first lie of the day.

'He came out,' said Louise excitedly. 'Just half an hour ago.'

'What?' said Mary.

'They made him lie down in the road,' Louise said. 'And then they handcuffed him. Like on the telly.'

'The children,' said Mary, clutching the back of the chair next to her. 'What about the children?'

'They came out too. He was carrying them. They lay down beside him, till Sharon called them.'

Mary sat down suddenly. 'She's safe.'

'She wasn't there,' Louise said scornfully. 'I told you. It was just the kids. She was outside.'

'He didn't kill them,' said Mary. 'They're all safe.'

'Pete says he'll go to prison,' Louise told her with relish. 'Bound to.'

'Oh God,' said Mary.

There was a creaking noise on the stairs.

'I'm off,' said Louise hurriedly. 'Tell Dad I left my project work behind or something. Tara.'

The last police car left around noon. As it swept through the estate it gave a final wail, brief and unnecessary. In her kitchen Mary heard it; the sound keened on, long after it had stopped, in her heart.

SERIOUSLY SEEKING J. K . GALBRAITH

My neighbour Babs had had them all: Clint Eastwood, David Essex, Richard Gere, Burt Reynolds . . .

Not really, you understand. In her dreams.

She used to describe the dreams to me, in shameless detail. And I found it entertaining, I suppose, in the old days. I squirmed at her choice of lovers – always glossy celebrities, tailor-made (at least in their day) for female fantasy – but squirming's not, in itself, unpleasurable. And I admired her courage in telling me – we were wives and mothers, after all; mature women, not dizzy teenagers.

She made the dreams sound impressively real. Not just new faces on the same body, going through the same motions. Richard Gere, apparently, had been touchingly shy and needed considerable encouragement, unlike David Essex who had seduced her with great panache in a field of sunflowers, and then danced naked with her through the flowers singing extracts from *The Sound of Music* (which hadn't seemed wrong at the time). And Burt Reynolds had had a curved scar on his hip that evoked in her the tenderest of emotions, somehow enhanced by his incapacity to utter more than a gruffly panted, 'Shit Babs,' throughout.

When Roger and I started divorce proceedings, however, I became a reluctant listener. Babs didn't, I'm sure, see that she was being tactless;

and maybe I was being oversensitive. They were only silly dreams, after all. And it must be hard for those who haven't experienced it to appreciate the sense of failure, including sexual failure, that accompanies even mutually agreed divorce.

But she assumed, I think, that everyone had dream lovers. Whether they admitted to them or not. She never challenged my denials, but from time to time she'd ask, almost sneakily, whom I'd like to dream about. 'If you could choose anyone,' she'd press. 'There must be someone.'

I normally ducked even this — not liking to admit, perhaps, that I honestly couldn't think of anyone. But on the day I received my divorce papers she asked me the question again — she was driving me home after a PTA meeting at the childrens' school — and a name simply popped out of my mouth.

'J.K. Galbraith,' I said, and had to take moment to adjust to this extraordinary thing I'd said. J. K. Galbraith? *J. K. Galbraith*? It took several seconds to mentally attach a face to the name. Then, encased in a ghostly rectangle that was undoubtedly my television set, his features appeared. The long laconic face, the intelligent, humorous eyes. Well yes, I thought, contemplating the vision, I did admire him; but not, surely, in that way? Yet having said it . . .

Babs had never heard of him. It was a relief. I explained, hurriedly, that he was an extremely tall American economist. And writer, diplomat, social commentator, oh all sorts of things. That I'd seen him on television, he'd had his own series once. 'Of course,' I said dismissively, 'he must be ancient by now.'

'That doesn't matter,' cried Babs, clearly delighted to have got a name, however obscure, out of me. 'He can be any age you like. As long as you can picture him. Why . . .' She went on to remind me that she dreamt about men who'd been dead for decades. Montgomery Clift after seeing a rerun of *Red River*, and James Dean any number of times.

That evening was the start of it. It was from then, the moment I realized that there was someone, a real person, for whom I felt desire and who was, in a sense, accessible, that I began to regret that for me, he wasn't. It was ridiculous of course, but such a small longing; and why should I be denied, even in my dreams? It made me start to view them as a whole, critically: at best humdrum, at worst exhaustingly anxiety-laden. No wonder nobody exotic chose to enter them.

Over the weeks the regret festered. I don't know why; maybe it was Bab's almost constant company, which was kindly intended, and for which in the main I was grateful; or maybe it was a mental displacement – an investment into this ultimately trivial regret of other, unacknowledged and perhaps more fundamental, regrets. And then one evening, when I was round at Babs' house while her husband Albert was out, she recounted the details of a nocturnal triumph with Kevin Kline; and I found myself asking, in a casual, joky manner, how she did it. Did she, I wondered, have to concentrate on her lovers before falling alseep? Bang her head on the pillow intoning their name, whatever?

She screeched with laughter and said goodness no, it wasn't as easy as that. 'I wish it was. God, imagine . . .' She rolled her eyes with a grin, before shaking her head. 'I have to really fancy them. Seriously fancy them, I mean. And go on fancying them. It takes months, sometimes.'

I thought this reply disappointing at first, but afterwards realized it wasn't. All Babs was saying was that she couldn't consciously will lovers into her dreams. I could hardly have expected that. But she could assist them there, by 'really fancying' them, and persisting in 'really fancying' them. That is, by genuinely desiring them, and presumably thinking wishful and lustful thoughts about them, over a period of time. Dreams are just the way we think at night. It was merely overspill.

So if it worked for her, it might work for me. It's hard to describe the excitement this stirred in me. I walked dazedly round my sitting-room for several minutes, absorbing it. I didn't have a problem with genuinely desiring J.K., I was sure. When I visualized him now I experienced intense, unmistakeable yearnings. But what I did have difficulty with was in holding him there long enough to have wishful or lustful thoughts about him. In its free-ranging state my mind was much more likely to dwell on the disgraceful antics of divorce solicitors, or wrangles about child support payments, or money worries generally, than on sex.

Here, however, fate stepped in. A week later I was in the County Library and on my way to the Legal section found myself passing Economics. My gaze fell on a collection of J.K.'s books; and on inspection one, *The Great Crash*, had a large close-up photograph of him on the back. Sitting in a relaxed deckchair attitude, grinning broadly, and looking spectacularly young (well, fiftyish) and handsome.

This, it suddenly came to me, was exactly what I needed. In a state close to elation I took two photocopies of the picture, recklessly abandoned my search for *Divorce made Painless* and hurried home.

I knew instinctively – or thought I did – what to do next. Before I went to bed that night I blu-tacked one copy above my pillow and the other on the adjacent wall, where I could see it from a lying position. Then lowered the bedside lamp to the floor, so the room was dimmed but not dark, and with my eyes turned towards the picture, went to sleep.

I did dream, but not about J.K. I dreamt I'd won the jackpot, in the form of sheets of five-pound notes, on a machine identical in every respect to the photocopier in the library. A pleasant dream, but not the right dream.

I unstuck the pictures and hid them away the next day – in case Babs saw them, during one of her unannounced and often roaming visits – but the following night repeated the performance; and this time dreamt that my solicitor and my ex-husband's solicitor were up in court, being tried for living off immoral earnings. The judge was just donning his black cap as I woke up.

I decided that the reason visual stimulus wasn't working was because in sleep one's eyes are closed. The general approach, though, on the evidence – both clearly wish-fulfilment dreams – still seemed promising. Maybe auditory stimulus could focus things more accurately.

I gave ways and means some thought overnight and the next day, when I had planned going into town anyway, I nipped into Woolworths and on the advice of an unusually helpful girl assistant – I told her I had a short speech to rehearse – bought a blank 'C15' audiotape. I went home and then after lunch, but before the children returned from school, I shut myself in the back sitting-room with the telephone off the hook and used my daughter's cassette player to record myself saying, 'You are dreaming about J. K. Galbraith,' on both sides of the tape. After supper I told my daughter I wanted to borrow the player to listen to music in bed, and last thing at night inserted the tape, and set it for continuous play.

But I couldn't get to sleep. My tone of voice, during the half-hour recording session, had degenerated most unfortunately, from a persuasive breathiness to dreary monotone, and was so irritating that I found myself snarling, 'No I'm bloody not,' at intervals back to it. At 2.30 a.m. I switched off the machine and subsequently dreamt about trying to push my way through a crowd of very tall people (none of whom was J.K.) and saying, 'Excuse me, excuse me,' as I struggled to reach my destination. The nature of this remains a mystery, since I never reached it.

I met Babs the following weekend in the spectators' gallery of the local swimming pool. As we watched and waved to our children below she told me that on the Friday she had spent a night of sexual enchantment with Stefan Edberg. It was a fortnight after he'd become Wimbledon champion.

'He brought the trophy with him,' she laughed, almost falling on top of me with amusement, 'God, what a hoot.'

I snapped, 'Christ Babs, he looks about twelve,' suddenly very angry. It was grossly unfair. She had Albert and all these bloody dream lovers, and I had no one. I didn't wait to have coffee with her after the children had changed, but invented a difficult casserole and drove home vicious with frustration.

The answer, I decided when I'd calmed down, was to steep myself in J.K. I'd been trying to take short cuts; idiotic short cuts, at that. It wouldn't do.

I returned to the library on the Monday and in purposeful but newly disciplined mood took out J.K.'s *Affluent Society* and *A View From the Stands*. The latter – a collection of his short writings – is a fairly weighty tome; the mere act of carrying it home felt virtuously penitential.

Over the next three weeks I read both books from cover to cover, including the copious footnotes, and had no dreams – to my waking recollection – of any significance at all. I learnt, however, among many other less personal facts, that J.K. was Canadian-born, which explained the delicious modulations of his American accent; and – this was more a reminder – that he had a well-developed, if ponderous, sense of humour.

By the end of the three weeks, although I hadn't yet dreamt about J.K., my mood was hugely improved. J.K. is essentially a man of letters; and there I was, already steeped in close to a million of them. His image was now rarely out of my waking thoughts; it was only a matter of time, I was confident, before he crossed the barrier into my dreams. I took the books back to the library and got out *The Anatomy of Power* and *The Age of Uncertainty*.

I had a dream – oh so close – that very night. I dreamt I was in hospital, but not as a patient; I was either a medical student or a nurse. Whichever, I had a white gown on and I was alone in some sort of changing room – my day clothes hung from a peg nearby – and I was waiting for the consultant to turn up. I thought of him as the consultant but of course really – and I knew this is in the dream – he was J.K. I actually heard his footfalls in the corridor, in the split second before my alarm clock woke me.

I was disappointed to have missed him, naturally, but above all reassured. I was going to dream about him. I was capable of it. And it would happen, very soon.

I was right. On the Saturday night, less than a week later, and only three chapters into *The Age of Uncertainty*, I finally dreamt about him.

In the dream I was lying in my bed at home, everything completely normal, as if settling down for a sleep, when there was a light knock at the door. 'Come in,' I said, and the door swung open. It was J.K. I said warningly, 'Mind your head,' (my bedroom door, like most, is only six foot six) and he gave me a grin, showing those wonderfully un-American imperfect teeth, ducked under the doorway and strode lopingly over to the foot of the bed.

I felt, I recall, neither shy, nor overly triumphant. More as a wife might, on the return from some overlong trip of her beloved husband. I snuggled down deeper into the bed and watched him take off his suit jacket.

'Sorry I'm late,' he said, in that scrumptious drawl of his, and laid the jacket neatly on the chair. He glanced over to the bed with a smile, loosening his tie.

I smiled back at him, in vast contentment. He walked round to the other side of the bed and lowered himself to sit on the cover.

I tilted my head towards him. As I did so a giddy incomprehension overcame me. There was a hump in the bed, between him and myself. A human hump. I followed it up, past a froth of pink lace spilling onto the covers, and found a face. It was Babs, lying beside me, her plump white arms outstretched in welcome.

J.K. murmured, 'Baby,' bending towards her, and she drew him to her bosom, with a cooing sigh.

Neither of them seemed to notice me. I lay a moment staring at the blank wall opposite, and then I woke up.

Biographical Note

Catherine Merriman was born in 1949 and brought up in London and Sussex. She studied statistics and sociology at the University of Kent, and in 1970 married her present husband Chris. For five years she worked for the Government Statistical Service, first in London and then in South Wales.

Apart from a 20,000 word novel at the age of twelve, Catherine did no creative writing until 1985. She has since had short stories published in Welsh, English and American magazines, and has also had non-fiction and poetry published.

She has had a variety of jobs, from barmaiding to teaching women's studies, but now works for the environmental organization Ecoropa, and as a volunteer worker for her local Women's Aid group. For the last eighteen years she and her husband have lived in a hillside village outside Brynmawr in Gwent. They have two teenage children, several pets and three motorbikes.

HONNO – The Welsh Women's Press

Honno has been set up by a group of women who feel that women in Wales have limited access to literature which relates specifically to them. The aim is to publish all kinds of books by women, in both English and Welsh including:

fiction, poetry, plays, children's books
research on Welsh women's history and culture
reprints of out-of-print titles.

Honno is registered as a community co-operative. Any profit will go towards future publications. Shareholders' liability is limited to the amount invested. So far we have raised capital by selling shares at £5 each to more than 300 women from all over Wales and beyond. We hope that many more women will be able to help us in this way. Buy as many as you can – we need your support. Each shareholder regardless of number of shares held, will have her say in the company and one vote at the AGM. Although shareholding is restricted to women, we welcome gifts and loans of money from anyone. If you would like to buy some shares or if you would like more information, write to: Honno 'Ailsa Craig' Heol y Cawl Dinas Powys De Morgannwg CF6 4AH.